THE PINNACLE

An earlier version of 'The White Trout' appeared in Edition 91 of *Fly-
life* Magazine.

National Library of Australia Cataloguing-in-Publication entry
Bovill, Lindsay
The Pinnacle
First edition
ISBN 978-0-6458795-2-0 (paperback)

Cover design by Lindsay Bovill and Lucinda Francis
Cover Photograph: Lake Pamamaroo, NSW, Australia (author)
All artwork within this book was created using original photographs
by Lucinda Francis and Lindsay Bovill

Email: lindsaybovill@gmail.com
Website: lindsaybovill.com

 A catalogue record for this
NATIONAL   book is available from the
LIBRARY   National Library of Australia
OF AUSTRALIA

THE PINNACLE

LINDSAY BOVILL

Dedication

For my beautiful Lucy:

It is a privilege to explore the rivers, deserts, backroads and remote trails of Australia by your side. I cherish our constant companionship through rain, dust, mud, starlight and firelight. With every new day I learn so much from you and about you. I am so grateful for every moment we share together.

Lake Numalla

Author's note

Although every fictional story in this collection relates to a single river, the short autobiographical 'vignettes' spaced between the fictional pieces are lived experiences drawn from different rivers across the continent.

Contents

Dedication   v
Author's note   vii

Preface (Vignette): Headwaters   1
WADDI   6
Vignette: Desert River   25
REMIGE   28
Vignette: A Dry Riverbed   43
JIMS RIVER   47
Vignette: 3x One River   54
THE WHITE TROUT   58
Vignette: Bull Rock   69
THE PINNACLE   73
Vignette: Black Sky   81
THE WADER   84
Vignette: Brookie   100
ORISON/DELTA   105

Acknowledgements   112

About the Author   114

Preface (Vignette):
Headwaters

I know the last days will be here, when the Sun runs into the ocean, and that I will see in a movement of sea birds and hear in the sound of water beating against the Earth what I now only imagine, that the ocean has a sadness beyond even the sadness of birds, that in the running into it of rivers is the weeping of the Earth for what is lost.

Barry Lopez, *River Notes*

Headwaters

H e had never seen a river like this one before.
Not in real life.

Not up close.

.

We were in the Great Dividing Range of Victoria, a vast sweep of mountains in Australia's South that extends far into the North, right up to the top of the continent. Our camping spot in a small clearing amongst the trees afforded an aerial view of a large, sinuous stretch of river, and we'd been watching it all day for tiny pricks of light, or water behaving like it shouldn't, or slight disturbances: any of which might indicate movement- *life*- beneath the surface.

Each day at dusk we would wind our way down the hill toward the water: just to be with it, to feel the cobbles underfoot, to take in the sweep of our favourite bend as the water coursed southward, undercutting a bank of blackwood and fern.

Back then he was a five year old. Rivers like this one- rivers that hold low through forests, rivers with beautifully cobbled streambeds and banks, rivers alive with birdsong and sparkling with insect wings- were an entirely new world to inhabit: a dreamscape. Meeting a river like this for the first time is less like a homecoming, and more a revelation of what home could mean.

Even back then, I think he somehow intuitively knew that.

.

One evening we were drawing near the water as usual: carefully, silently, with the same vigilance one employs when trying to approach an animal unseen. I hung back and let him go onwards, watching him sneak all the way up to the edge- as if becoming known to the river might cause it to behave differently- where he squat down, beginning to absorb the riverscape. For long minutes he focused on the water passing in front of him, the wavelets reflecting the pastels of evening, glides and riffles introducing him to the language of turbulent and laminar flow. After a time, I moved up beside him so we could watch quietly together.

Then: a blindside, double-barrelled. He broke the long silence by asking how old the river was, and if rivers ever die. Derailed, I explained my thoughts as best I could, unable to form any worthwhile response that could adequately match the gravity of the question I'd been totally unprepared for.

A few more minutes of silence passed. I stood transfixed at the question. He sat transfixed at the water. A kingfisher flicked past. Mayflies danced. Rocks radiated stored Autumn sunlight. The eucalypts were still. He remained there, the whole while, watching the water flow.

Finally, eventually, he broke the silence.

"One day, when we are old," he promised in a quiet voice, as twilight gathered in the stream, "we are going to come back to this river and tell it that we love it."

WADDI

Waddi, Birdsville

There is a gap between what is us and what is not, and names are, literally, the terms with which we negotiate the distance...names are a way that the mind and even the heart make an elemental kind of contact with the world and come to establish a form of intimacy with it.

Ted Leeson, *Jerusalem Creek*

How many ways are there of looking at a landscape?

Jan DeBlieu, *Wind*

I wasn't always like this.

I never had arthritic, creaking limbs. I've rarely shed as much bark as I do these days.

Deep furrows course like dry creek beds up the height of my trunk.

.

Old age is seeping into me, encircling me, rising up from the darkness beneath, breaching into daylight. It's gotten past the mycorrhizae, past the baking gibber, past the soil microbes, and now envelopes me: senescence morphing me into something more clarified, more distilled. I've grown hard with time, brittle with experience. I know that every year passing without fire brings me one year closer to being burned alive by a lightning bolt, a wildfire, a discarded cigarette butt.

.

People think of trees as being rooted in one place: stationary, fixed. Manacled. But I've seen the people who come to look at me, or who drive past without stopping, or who break off pieces of me to possess as souvenirs or trophies or convenient fire kindling. Of them all, I rarely see one who ever appreciated what true freedom, true mobility is: who knew how to employ the art of movement to shift through the world in a purposeful and meaningful way. My idea of freedom is different, though: I don't need to leave my home in order to become worldly. I can picture the whole sweep of humanity right from where I am. I sense everything, the entire immensity of human diversity. It comes to me here in the stony heart of the Australian desert from across the oceans and fields and cities of the globe: the spilling of cultures into and across the land, ten thousand languages blended and scattered upon the winds of the world.

.

I represent a quantity beyond human comprehension (much like geological deep-time: much like the speed of light). The tourist information billboard nearby puts my age at something most people have trouble believing. It's a guess though, really: a shot in the dark. Nobody knows our age except us, and to us, time moves differently anyway. We Waddi have no use for the ritual tallying of years. Rather, we take advantage of seasons, or environmental conditions, wherever and however we might find them. We put forth fruit in times of plenty. Our seeds follow suit. Thorns are deployed when we are most vulnerable. We, as opposed to the humans we observe, measure time not by moments passing.

We measure it by opportunities to grow.

.

In the speech of my human visitors- in their manner and deportment, in the various degrees to which each defers to others for guidance and acknowledges what is unknowable- I can visit the lands and cultures from which each person has originated. I can locate their ancestry by the parsing of a sentence, the phraseology, the distinct way the tongue moves against the palate, the way the hands are employed for emphasis. I learn what is most important to them as individuals within a society, and through these observations learn about the universe of human variegation. The scraps of wind-borne sound I capture and filter from far off continents- this is useful too, yes- but only partially. It is a mismatch of confused dialects, 8 billion radio frequencies all tuned in at once, impossible to disentangle, distorted by atmospheric turbulence. But when people come to visit- when they are right here in front of me- these are the same languages I recognise, and learn over time to comprehend.

In my lifetime of listening to the peoples of the world, what has struck me as most reassuring is the different ways each culture senses and interprets landscapes. I've learnt there are as many versions of a landscape as there are people to witness it, trees to grow in it, bacteria to flourish on it, animals to navigate it. There are of course overlaps too extensive to mention: but these all relate to general, obvious things. It is the small dissimilarities which surprise me over and again: nuanced conflicts of understanding that seem to hold disproportional weight, variations which shift the moral, ethical, intrinsic centre of gravity. These slight differences, to me, are the things that matter the most: the spaces between worlds which hold the most significance.

History- linguistic, political, cultural, intercultural, environmental, emotional- seems to dictate exactly what it is that people notice about me, about the other Waddi's, about the land around me. Landscapes are the bedrock of language, and I can feel the contour, the colour, the sounds of far-off places in the words of my human visitors. I have learnt there are a hundred other words employed to describe phyllodes: *leaves, needles, navch, lapu, piguttuk, patta.* For each inflorescence, there are ten thousand ways to describe a flower: *tsvetok. Fiore. Bloem. Imrali.* I hear them as a mother points my boughs out to a child, or as photographers discuss how far they can push their f-stop and still capture the dull glint of reflected sunlight from my cuticles. These names (words spoken, words thought) collide with my flesh and embed, permanently reminding me there is more than one way to view the world, a culture, an unassuming flower on a tree, a slight wind on the nape of the neck, the smell of rain on rock. Through this I have become aware that every single experience is as a rainbow: the impressions of any two people, any two cultures, will never be the same, will always at some point be distinguishable.

I sense both a beauty and an inherent danger to this patterning of interpretation: for no single culture has ever come close to providing adequate meaning and insight to what I, and the land around me, fundamentally *is.* It has taken them all to get somewhere close, but the qualities they detect are never focussed into a single, coherent image. To create the most meaningful impression of the whole, all these multitude of viewpoints must be coalesced, fused into a single point of white-hot light.

Without the total and absolute input of every society, and every individual voice within it, how can it be said that I am known?

.

Humans. I never really saw many of them until later in my life. Mainly other animals. Mainly birds. When I was younger I'd see a people- the Wangkangurru Yarluyandi- moving through the desert, often actively seeking out my kind: for the shade, for the birdlife, and sometimes for our flesh, our wood, for making war clubs. Waddi. We grow so slowly- our heartwood so dense and unyielding- that we made the best warclubs of all. Through us, fear and death were spread: across the land, across time, and across cultures. We also acted as vessels for transporting fire: our wood enabled embers to be safely nurtured on long journeys across the desert.

It always seemed ironic to me that beings of such immense age could be used to curtail the lives of some and advance the lives of others. In time though, our culture- the Waddi culture- learned to understand these different responsibilities. You might say we gained a unique perspective.

We are never, though, asked to share what we have learnt.

.

Most people I see these days move a lot faster than those a century ago: a paved road goes by here now, and only a small portion of the traffic pulls over to acknowledge me or my family. Some do stop, mainly because it's a convenient place to rest, or check for phone reception (there isn't any), or let out dogs and children. Some even read the information sign about us, and even fewer will walk a few steps beyond that, snap a picture, and then go on their way: either unfazed, impatient, or most dangerous of all, as fully informed experts.

It is not often I observe people being truly humbled in my presence.

.

Every now and then, though, I do receive the kind of attention I consider worthy. Not worthy of me, you understand: I'm talking about a manner of virtue appropriate for humans as a species.

It might be a child, or an adult, or maybe a person as furrowed and wrinkled as I am. This person will step from the car, move off a ways, and take a long, deep look at the landscape. Not just the trees. Not just the land. Not just the sky. They peel all of that back, are not deceived by the facade of the obvious. Like everyone else, they will notice the way galahs sit in pairs, and how the shadow of grass plays on the gibber. They will take in the distance and patterning of the Waddi's, the canopy shape, the degree to which we shade the ground. But they will sense movement and structure beyond this, intuitively, as if the immediately visible were a trick, a trap, a veneer superimposed upon another, more profoundly impenetrable landscape. I meet these people, when they come to me: and when I see them recognise that this deeper landscape is inherently unknowable, I am comforted that there is still hope for the world.

These people walk up to me, pause about a tree height away (I calculated this long ago and have learned to predict it), and watch me. They do not reflexively reach for their phones or cameras. As they watch- no, as they simply be, and exist, and pay *attention*- they learn how a slight wind patterns my flesh, take the time to experience the sight of birds riding out gusts in my limbs. They marvel at ants navigating the crevices in my bark, and note the small ways in which their behaviour is different to ants on other trees. They appreciate the way sunlight is filtered by my canopy in a very particular manner, observe how the outline of a Waddi can be eerily human, and wonder with some concern (all of them do) where all the young Waddi's are, the next generation. They try to imagine what was going on in the world when I was a seedling- which historical event was the closest to my birth- and in this they invariably fail, underestimating how old I really am.

They feel my needles, test their scent. They caress my bark slowly and from a place of deep respect, as if earning the trust of a horse. They stand and look up through my canopy, filtered and diffused light playing on their faces, a look of openness and awe etched into them. They might sit awhile, or sketch, or make a note, or just think. They might lay beneath me, eyes closed, and take in the sound of the sifting wind above. By their behaviour- by their words, movements, thoughts- they reveal themselves. After a long while they will leave like the others- they always must- but these people drive off slowly, looking back. And they do not forget.

These people hold a perpetual memory of what is important.

·

I have tried hard to identify a commonality amongst those who stop and spend a while with me. There is a unique thread that runs between them all. I have learned to sense it as a river of doubt, a discord that defines them as individuals and flows through them as a group of people: their respect for the natural world is at once calm and urgent, headlong and measured, mournful and exuberant. The things they learn and experience are often so incredible, so implausible, that they are wary of sharing it with strangers for fear of being confirmed a pariah. Partly because of this, they are circumspect towards most aspects of human society. They worry about the natural world around them- intensely- and in their quiet solastalgia wonder just how much they, and the land, can take. They grieve the knowledge that their children won't be aware of what is now missing from the landscape.

These people- I recognise them from all countries, all cultures on the globe- are burdened, and humbled, by the simple things they find in the world around them.

.

I have also learnt that all lands and cultures are encumbered by counting within their ranks the entitled, the greedy, the unethical, the ill-considered. I have learnt to locate these people in a particular way, by looking for very precise mannerisms: for example, the way graceful things- deep silence, happiness in others, innocent wonder- are instantly crushed by them. For these people it turns out that it is beauty, of all possible intimidations, which is most intolerable. Through them I've learnt to expect the verbal desecration of all history, the active choice not to be kind, and the relentless belittling of things that really matter: the ridiculing of simple pleasures, the erosion of any sign of uncomplicated trust, and the dismissal of small acts of generosity. These people form the distracted, the emotionally invulnerable, the extrinsically gluttonous from every part of the planet.

I see menace in the way these people act. But what I hear is far worse, a threat not limited to any one group, society, or culture: a threat that exists beyond any single intention, one that lives outside of morality. I detect, in the parlance of humans as a species, the trend towards a global precariousness: a degradation of articulation, of the ability to share and communicate what is valued. I have already seen this lead to misunderstanding, apathy, and policies of focussed destruction: of places, thoughts, people, and cultures not immediately useful or profitable. I hear the weathering of language from other lands, coming in on the wind, and I hear it on the continent all around me. The final consequence of this is the obliteration of the natural world: its animals, its geology, its dark skies, its quiet spaces, the endless ways in which to interpret it all. Linguistic decay leading to mass destruction: by gradual acquisitiveness, by blatant economic depredation, by the en-masse deprivation of access to knowledge and words that describe what is intrinsically precious.

To defend what is irreplaceable, people need to tell whoever will listen- and whoever will not- about the specifics, the nuances, of whatever it is they feel we cannot afford to lose: those precise places or instances that resonate, for whatever reason, with the heart. To delineate, acutely and with the finest possible resolution, the most meticulous details of the place, the rock, the gully, bird, tree species, riverbend, moonlit landscape- to relate it from a location rooted so deeply in the heart that finding the right words is to reach inside and ablate a piece of the soul. To come from somewhere, become tethered to it with a stake, and, standing ground, defend this creek, this continent, this sacred location, this sky of silence and darkness, this idea or ideal or moral- defend it eloquently, passionately, and with utter ferocity- with a ruthlessness, an intolerance for intentional ignorance, an incessant linguistic fusillade designed to save the natural systems of this planet.

I have seen that to be successful at this on the scale I think is required, the entire vocabulary of the planet needs to be put to use. We need the dead languages too- the words and names each extinct society and language group once used to discuss and deal with threats of oblivion- but these are gone now, and we must speak knowing that many of the most appropriate terms and phrases have already vanished, and that the best we can do is to keep searching and asking, even as we mourn them. And, critically, we need to talk about nature with other cultures- especially those most foreign to us- and to reciprocate by listening more intently than we speak. The alternative- to blend the piquancy of Earth's peoples into a single permanent language with which to talk about nature and landscapes, create a single philosophy, a single emaciated vocabulary- would be to signal, and allow, the final destruction of the natural world.

In a world like that, there is no room for me. I do not exist.

...

Long ago- tens of thousands of millennia ago, longer than even I can comprehend- there were no trees here. This place was an inland sea filled with creatures who came, lived a while, and eventually- like all things- ended up extinct. These days though, the visible evidence for this past ocean is caught by only a very few eyes. Most people miss it. But those who slowly converse with the land, and recognise themselves as an alien moving through a foreign world, *always* see it: maybe a vertical rock displaying ripples of an ancient sea floor, or maybe a marine fossil high on an exposed, sunbeaten trail, or even- through the mere fact of my existence- the trapped groundwater deep below my roots, water locked into deep storage countless millennia ago.

I have another perspective on these ancient waters, one rarely- *never*- parsed in Journals or argued around Campfires. For I view the ancient collection of subterranean rainwater as among the true headwaters of most rivers on this continent, including The Pinnacle River. You haven't met The Pinnacle yet: but when you do, and when you wonder where the water within this stream originated, I urge you to credit me with a small- the tiniest- portion of that origin story.

Headwaters, I've learnt during my years on Earth, exist in time, throughout time, and isolated from time.

They are their own pulse, with their own heartbeat.

.

Long before I was here, the rainwaters washing Gondwana entered the Eromanga Sea, carrying eroded material with them: sediments that, over time, accumulated and compressed to become the water-storing layers of the Great Artesian Basin. You might say- and it is not a stretch to do so- that water formed its own storage vessel: the water from the Sea became trapped when the porous rock was eventually capped by further depositions of sediment. Today, groundwater trapped within this aquifer has few places to naturally escape: and where it does, it erupts out of the ground at temperatures beyond boiling. In other places, it seeps through the rock, entering subsurface paleochannels, where, as good fortune would have it, some of us Waddi have discovered it with our roots, and have so formed communities. From there, this millions-of-years journey of water molecules culminates in transportation via xylem to engage in some or other cellular process, finally exiting our bodies through stomata, to be whisked away by wind and thermal currents tens or hundreds or thousands of kilometres away: and, if the atmospheric conditions are dialled in just right, some very small percentage of it shall eventually end up in the Pinnacle River watershed. Sure, water from a million other sources dwarfs those few molecules I contribute: but my water, though small in volume, does have the distinction of having travelled among the furthest distances to be there.

So, when I claim that an ancient sea can be the true headwater of a modern river, I'd like to think my long view is at least partially correct.

.

In my life I have seen the land around me flourish, wither, bloom, burn. But the background noise of natural systems and civilisations deteriorating has, in recent times, become a reverberant, piercing resonance I can barely endure, and no longer know how to block out. Chemical intrusion of Artesian groundwater. Intentional desecration of sacred places. The upturned snowglobe of airborne pollutants circulating, descending, sifting by like mist. Polyfluoroalkyl and perfluoroalkyl in every living thing.

Life in nature's harshest environments has never been easy. I am used to witnessing death, pain, despair. So many times here, deep in the baking desert of the Australian interior, I've witnessed scorching air suck the life out of creatures seeking reprieve in the relief of my shade, when all I was ever really offering them was a quiet place to die alone. Animals, humans.

Their flesh never lasts long, their bones eventually reclaimed by the land- scattered, windblasted by sand particles- their knowledge and memories disappearing with them. But the scale at which I see entire natural systems degrading: this now dwarfs any individual human loss. To lose a person is heartbreaking, but to lose entire cultures and environments due to conscious avarice and callousness: this, to me, is epochal. Species defining. It's a degree of global instability I don't think I've ever been aware of.

...

For a while now I've been noticing, more than normal, the disintegrating, collapsing flesh of my kind around me. It takes a long time for a Waddi to break down completely, but it happens eventually, the last molecule broken up, ingested, drawn off by the wind, leaving nothing behind. We, too, perish in the shade of our kin. And I know I can't be all that far off, if I'm honest, from journeying down that slow road myself. That is why I feel now it is time for me to speak up.

I've been paying attention all my life: always open to suggestion, to new things. Learning from each person that visits me, each culture. So my summation of what I've learnt is, I think, a valuable thing to hear. If only for what it is. Discard it if you want. Or, keep it. It's of no use to me any more. It can only be of use to you.

What I have been waiting to see all these years- all these decades and centuries- is the pooling together of human knowledge, ideas, unknowns. For people of different cultures to find common ground, no matter how tenuous, upon which to intersect. There are many worlds that come to my corner of the desert, many moralities, ideas, ethics, all accumulating across time beneath my boughs, only very narrowly missing the knowledge, experiences, and histories of those who have visited before them.

It is too easy for each person to possess an honest sense of having been informed, of having gained a unique insight. What I want to see is those understandings discarded, entwined, respectfully eviscerated, and in all cases spliced with the endless other ways of viewing the world, my world, to grow and guard against those who would visit harm upon all cultures: the vast and interdependent cultures of humanity, of trees, of the animals, of the fungi and Archaea, of the forms of life we are yet to realise exist.

I want to see the anabatic flow of ideas.

.

For me, the Pinnacle River is important because so few people who are familiar with it are also familiar with me. I'm simply too far away, perceived as too insignificant. This is very dangerous. I want to send a message that even the unseen, the unimagined, the distant and removed, can readily knit into and influence far away places and lives. I want for people to plunge their whole bodies into The Pinnacle, to lay on its cobbled bottom, to open their eyes, their ears, become aware of hygrosensation, equilibrioception, consciously make calculations based upon a literacy of buoyancy, pressure, gravity: to look upstream and parse the current so minutely that the origin story of every water molecule can be learnt- comet, aquifer, Electron Transport Chain, transpiration, bladder, snowmelt, blood- and understand, as the water is rushing past, that places like this are not static, or predetermined, or destined, but formed of components in an intricate flux so complex, so beyond comprehension, that any form of analysis involving reductionism, or executive summary, or oversimplification, is to play an active, conscious role in the destruction of beauty.

.

I have learnt, over the centuries, that as human societies and cultures cleave and dissolve, disintegration of the moral landscape is always close, tethered, flittering in the slipstream. People know this. The cultures on this planet have always guarded heavily against external (and internal) corrosive forces: new ideas, new temptations, new technologies and ways of knowing. Threats. Outsiders. Things that might alter a fundamental foundation, a Certain Knowledge. And I see very clearly now the major fault of humanity: the failure to embrace the idea that culture remains unfulfilled and incomplete unless it is shared and built upon.

As one of this continent's oldest organisms, I have seen, on occasion, the extraordinary happen when people of different cultures, different backgrounds, work together: offering wisdom, asking advice, sharing methods of vigilance. I've learnt that working together does not mean homogenisation: it means integration and overlap, for which variation is fundamentally required. I've also come to appreciate that we cannot survive where this human-driven planet is going without these variations cohabiting.

There exists an urgency to converge, listen openly to each person, each culture, and forge a path ahead propelled by a fearless, unfaltering knitting together of the best each has to offer: a path to answers, and to questions, coalesced by a requirement not just to survive, but to fiercely exist in the face of imminent existential threat.

I have seen enough in my years- through the people I have known- to hold a genuine optimism for the human world. I have faith that people- from different places, diverse backgrounds, people with different experiences, who know how much there is to lose- will draw together, each say what he has seen, learnt, and lost: and, that others will listen. Listen, and know how to protect and nurture the things they hear: cradle them in the hand like hot fragments shed from a meteor, exhaling breath to keep them lucent, energised, alive, until they return to their own families, communities, cultures, worlds as diverse as there are places to exist in, to offer the glowing embers to minds as receptive to fire as desiccated eucalypt kindling.

I hope, when this happens, it will not be too late for them.

Sturt National Park

Vignette: Desert River

We had spent more than two years planning this expedition: a journey deep into the Australian desert, one that would see us trace the trails of historical explorers, experience the thrill of finding centuries-old flintknapped tools, and become exposed to new landscapes that felt, upon entering them, like returning home to a place we had never before even imagined.

To get to our first camp, we endured days of vehicle-shuddering, nerve-shattering backroads: hard hours of long, intense concentration, and crippling terror, resignation, focus, pure joy, isolation, and a cold self-reliance that either does, or does not, get you into and out of places like this alive and safe.

And then we arrive: the engine is cut. We get out, ten yards from our home for the next week: a remote desert river, so wide and slow at this point that it effectively forms one large, long, endless waterhole.

The shift from oppressive and constant stress to total tranquility was so sudden we felt physically and mentally crushed by it. This sensation- part relief and part vacuum- was not to be found solely in the cessation of stressors, but in the release experienced in the abrupt switch to total immersion in a natural environment: the demanding, exhausting journey we'd endured was nothing compared to the aural and visual assault that leached into our awareness the instant the engine was killed. The gentle breeze (so gentle) in the long, waxed eucalypt leaves; the symposiae of a dozen new species of birds, their calls stitching together the languid afternoon air, penetrating the atmosphere and binding it together with threads of music, in order it might be protected and contained; the tindered savannah, grass and trees all granite-still, guarded, waiting to see what kinds of people these new intruders might prove to be before exhaling and resuming their day as trees and rocks.

All these elements of landscape- sky, bird, desert river, wavering light, birdsong- blended into an all-encompassing, all pervasive calm.

There, by the river, in that desert, on that day, we discovered a species of peace we never knew could possibly exist.

REMIGE

Lake Numalla

The bird out of place is always the first to die.

J. A. Baker, *The Peregrine*

In November, just before she died, Justine had made her wishes clear regarding her sketchbook. She instructed her parents to choose somebody to pass it on to: someone that could be trusted to keep it safe, perhaps add to it, and in turn make a similar decision in the future about handing it on. She wanted the book preserved: it was, Justine believed, her true essence, the most tangible and irreducible part of her.

She'd started on the book back in the early stages: back when a slim hope still existed for her. Hefty with thick pages, the cover was a deeply tanned full-grained leather, a single gold flower embossed in one corner. The paper was clean, textured, and off-white. She had relished the smell of the leather, and often thumbed the countersunk cotton side-stitching when in deep thought.

They had moved up from another part of the state a few years before, so she could finish high school in an area with forest nearby: she'd wanted to gain experience volunteering with park rangers in the Summer. It was only in the year following graduation that she became ill. The trajectory of her disease would follow the outline of one of the nearby mountains she had helped keep free of weeds: flat at the top, leading to a gentle downwards slope, then exponentially decreasing to a vertical precipice, ending in an abrupt stop at the valley floor.

.

The first sketch Justine had made in the book was of a dead mopoke owl. The three of them- mum, dad and her- were driving home from one of the initial specialist visits when she spotted the bird on the road. *Pull over*, she had firmly instructed. The sense of authority and urgency was unmistakable.

She had not been asking.

Justine got out and ran to the owl before the car had fully slowed, arraying the pencils on the tarmac, studying the bird from every angle. She put her nose to the bird, to the road, stroked the bird with the back of her fingers, spoke softly to it. Finally, she lay in the road and sketched it. Her father had panicked and urged her to get up- it wasn't safe- but her mother looked at him, a sharp, hollow conveyance which read *Please, give her this?* And so he'd made sure passing cars slowed, waving them on as they gawked and offered insults.

For the most part it was silent though, save for the constant reassurance of the Pinnacle River just beyond the road.

Justine had sketched obliviously, aware only of the bird on the bitumen before her. Finally she stood, moving the bird to some roadside weeds, laying it in a patch of blue forget-me-nots. She kissed her index finger and pressed it to the breast of the mopoke. "Sorry, owl. I'm so sorry." Then she walked back to the car, sat down, and began a deep, inconsolable sobbing.

.

Justine had been dead for some months before the mopoke sketch again lay open to the light and mountain air. Her parents had not been able to bear exposing themselves to the company of the book until this point: but they saw it as the only way to inject any meaning into the first birthday following her death.

Carol and Dan were not the only ones who knew Justine as a terrible drawer at best. People had always made light of this, joking with her openly about it. Justine herself used to laugh at her own inability to draw simple items. Once, in the short months before she died, Justine was asked to draw a picture of a house for one of her younger cousins, and it looked awful, worse than the pre-schooler could have done himself. It was probably the last thing she ever laughed about, and the last thing they all laughed about together.

But this comical lack of ability was not reflected in her sketchbook. The first three pages contained a variety of anatomical studies of the mopoke of such accuracy and quality that at first her parents did not trust it was her own work. The pencil rendering of a single feather on the tarmac appeared as delicate and soft as a real-life semiplume. The scaled legs, the bloodied chest, the broken head with a single lifeless eye staring from the surface of the paper. The insinuation of a life having left the husk of the defeated form. The recognition of grace and beauty amidst brutal circumstances. The sketches were frightening, and promoted unease, yet they were also calming, and electric with a kind of distilled hope. They were depicted so perfectly lifelike, the detail so exquisitely executed, that certainly, Dan suggested, they beheld somebody else's sketchbook. They almost missed the evidence confirming it as Justine's own work, an inscription she had made with a 4B pencil: *Owl on road. Blue flowers, ditch. Pinnacle close by.*

.

On that first day, they did not turn through the rest of the book page by page, but opened up the book randomly- trying to prove (though never voice) that the mopoke drawings were an anomaly. So to a fresh page: a black falcon, sketched as it had appeared shooting past them. They remembered this: it had been a blur to them, a black dart fired from the clouds one day near an oak grove. Justine had managed to capture the bird in such a way that it could not have been any other type of falcon: she had managed, in her sketch, to catch the line and purpose of its trajectory. "*Pigeons feeding, Falco subniger*" was the simple scrawl.

Another page: a blackbird with tattered feathers drinking from the cats' water bowl. It must have been sketched from her bedroom window. And others: sparkling Pinnacle water reflected from the undersides of riparian vegetation through the beech trees across the yard. A lyrebird disappearing into a shrub at the edge of a trail, drawn as the otherworldly shadow that lyrebirds often are.

Whenever she'd drawn, her parents had not looked over her shoulder. They sensed it was private and important, so left her alone.

The fact they'd never applauded the impossible talents of their daughter now tore at them.

.

Over the next year or so, they discovered a way to move through the book. One fresh set of drawings every week, working from front to back. Sometimes the topic took up one page only, on other occasions several. Each Saturday they would pack a lunch, and hike to the Mt Pinnacle summit, and there sit and look out at the view, watch the clouds, listen to the birds. They would try and hear what scraps of information the wind carried: a cropduster taking off from the valley floor, the whistling calls of Wedge Tails, a passing tourist complaining about phone reception. Then, when they sensed the moment was right, they would open up the sketchbook and turn to the bookmark. What would it be today? A raptor with a galaxiid perched on a fencepost? A swallow gathering cobwebs and insects off the dead pine tree near the long glide? A heron, trying its hardest to impersonate a shattered stump? A fox crossing a field clutching a rooster? Nothing was predictable, nothing was ordinary. And, as the weeks progressed, and they moved through the book, they began to notice something.

As her illness advanced, Justine's drawings gradually took on a quality of perspective that rose, slowly, to a record of natural history never before achieved in its sophistication. Her sketches, as both the pages and her time on Earth ground down, became ever more penetrating in their awareness, more incisive in their rendering, her perception growing more acute. The fox with the rooster, which was seen from behind for about 30 seconds one morning as it fled the yard, for instance: this moment was sketched from the riparian perspective of a small wooden stile by a boggy ditch the fox negotiated nearly one hundred yards away. The stile was in the immediate foreground, the fox leaping over it, the bird limp in its jaws. The fox's eyes were fixed on its landing point on the shore, the grass and weeds strong against a slight breeze, and in the distance the three of them could be seen in the yard, pointing at the fox. The rooster was beautifully rendered, its sickles caught by the wind, saliva-stained hackles stiff near the fox's mouth, the limp body of the bird following the same path through space as the fox. Justine had never held any interest in foxes: had never studied one up close, or paid much interest to their behaviour. But she had captured the very marrow of the fox, the essence of it: she seemed to sense something seeping out through its skin, informing the shape and texture of the fur, the sharp eyes, the acceptance of a lifelong persecution by humans, an adaptability and intelligence and resourcefulness seeping directly from the fox's cells, its DNA, its every past experience and memory.

It continued on, week by week, each sketch more subtle and perceptive than the last, accomplishing more with less pencil, though somehow containing more detail. Over the months that she sketched, Justine became able, with a flourish of her pencil, to render scenes not visible on timescales discernible to humans: only to high speed photography, only to eyes peering through an additional lens of a lifetime of studying wildlife. She had found, it seemed, some other way to access insights to the natural world around her, a kind of knowing that was, finally, animalistic.

It seemed that each drawing served, for Justine, as a remige. As the sketches accumulated, the world opened up, offering insight, providing escape, perspective, rising above what her own experiences and senses could access in order to *see*, to record the natural world around her. It seemed that this phenomenon was not restricted to drawing birds: but only if it was birds that formed the theme of the drawing.

It was difficult for her parents, working out what to do with that sketchbook. They felt it belonged in a museum, or a gallery, but did not want to part with it (not that permanently, not that flippantly), or see it fall within the control of a Society or Government Institution. The idea crossed their mind to offer it momentarily to a psychologist, or biologist, even a forensic pathologist at one point, but each time they pulled back, not wanting the work subjected to external dissection, scrutiny, or opinion. They asked Justine's friends- they had shown some of them, the closest ones- and they suggested photographing each page and placing it all on the internet as a memorial to Justine. But this idea didn't sit right either, so they let it quietly fade.

In the end, they came to a simple decision: the only entity that could be entrusted with something so sacred as the sketchbook, they believed, was The Pinnacle River itself.

It had been there all along with them, in some way or another, the whole time.

.

On the year of what would have been her 20th birthday, a backpack was filled with supplies- thermos (coffee), sandwiches (egg & lettuce), home-made biscuits, and fruit, and chocolate, and water. Carol and Dan had struck off early in the morning, on foot, for the Pinnacle: searching for a place where the river coincided with the deepest possible section of forest. Contour maps had told them half the story- had helped narrow it down some- but it would still take lots of hiking and searching to stumble upon the right place, the *only* right place. They knew the location would reveal itself when it was found.

Every now and then, they thought they had it: one time it was a large boulder encircled by eucalypts, a quiet place with mossy logs and wrens all around. But it did not seem definitive enough: it seemed too cliche. Something important was lacking. So, they searched on.

At one point, they heard the Pinnacle not far off. Here, the channel was only a few yards wide, the bed cobbled, the edges firm. They headed towards it, refreshing their canteens, and realised the land was slowly darkening around them, the possibility of an approaching flash storm gripping the occasion with a sudden urgency. The wind had dulled to a cool breeze, and wrens began chatting on nearby boughs: a fox ran right past them, noticing but ignoring them. The forest slowly became one giant shadow: minute by minute, the light was leaching out of the land. Resigned to the fact they would soon be drenched in rain, Carol and Dan remained focussed.

In any case, there was no place here to take adequate shelter.

They were standing watching the scenery around them, trying to visually pierce it, trying to identify a way forward, when a small red feather floated by on the water in the dim light, spinning in the small eddies created by exposed boulders. It looked like it belonged to a Flame Robin.

Upstream, Justine's mother pointed.

It took them one hundred yards, but they found it. A goshawk was perched on a rock by the stream, eating the robin, both birds barely identifiable in the low light. Feathers were strewn everywhere. The hawk saw them, and withdrew into the forest depths: a shadow extracting itself, morphing into the shape and colour of the receding trees, melting into them, dragging the light of the understorey away with it, but leaving the Flame Robin behind.

Justine's parents approached the dead bird.

Here, they agreed.

Here was good.

.

Only now they noticed the other birds. Songbirds, mainly, but also magpies, crows, ravens. Singing, like at dusk. It began as a trickle, with those first few wrens, and within a few short minutes birdsong flooded the forest: the trilling, sifting, sparkling audible rainbow of crepuscular birdsong, working toward, it seemed, some kind of crescendo.

The book was removed from the backpack, opened, and turned to the very last page: a blank, crisp white. Carol sat on the ground, right next to the dead robin, with the book open on her lap. She reached down, selected a robin feather caught in a bracken frond, and sketched it best as she could, before signing her name and passing the book over to Dan, who did the same with a different feather.

When it was done, the feathers were slipped into the page as a bookmark, and the book closed for the very last time. A hole was fashioned next to the robin- shallow and handscraped- and the sketchbook placed within it. They moved fast. Soil back on top, then river rocks, one at a time, until a mound had been formed a foot high. There was now very little light to work with: when placing the final few stones, they had to work mainly by feel.

The birdsong had totally ceased, and all animal noise had fallen away into silence: all except insects and frogs, invisible by the river.

Their focus had been so intense that they missed the complete cessation of the wind.

.

Justine's parents stood by the small memorial, watching it in the gloom, waiting for the imminent downpour, prepared to get soaked to the bone if it meant they could stand there a while longer, keeping company by the cairn they knew they would probably never again try to locate. The sketches within it belonged to the river, belonged to the forest now: leaving it in peace seemed the only right thing to do.

Looking skywards for the first time in a long while, they saw what, at first glance, appeared to be stars: and, then, more of them. They even recognised constellations: Orion held the sky between two eucalypts.

"Oh my lord, Dan" breathed Carol, peering back behind them. "Look."

Dan slowly turned.

A perfect ring of fire hung in the sky. The corona of the Sun radiated outwards from a central black mass, dark as a dilated pupil, absent and lightless as an empty chair at the table. They stood humbled as the sky above burned, as the stars glistened, as the sharp air crackled with an unearthly, electric clarity, the forest silent beneath, the landscape all around laying in an induced state of night. Frogs called: bats clicked overhead. The freshly harvested stones on the cairn, still glistening with river water, reflected a soft, strange, translucent light from the eclipse.

The Moon slowly slid across the face of the Sun, an opaque nictitating membrane: light began to flood into the world again. The stars slowly vanished before them, released into a vast ocean of light, sinking into the depths of space like stones, as irretrievable as prayers. Slowly, one by one, the birds again began to sing: the songs of morning. Blackbirds, magpies, wrens, butcher birds. The call of a falcon. The frogs ceased, the bats slowly disappeared, a brisk wind picked up. Finally, eventually, full daylight once again reigned over the forest, and the world continued as if nothing of particular note had occurred.

Nearby, water molecules released from distant tributaries slid silently by, the Pinnacle voicing only when the flow was interrupted- by a branch lodged in the riverbed, a kingfisher breaking the surface film- or, when the gliding water, having negotiated the form of a partially submerged boulder, re-joined the main current.

Vignette: A Dry Riverbed

There had been no water in this desert riverbed for almost a year, with nothing likely to change for another half year at least. The droughts here come too often: animals die, plants die, outback stations die, people leave. Only the bones of the fallen remain: the place is implacably unwavering on this point.

The riverbed seemed to be waiting: for rain, for birds, for fish, for people to pay attention.

Instead of water flowing downstream, on this day heat flowed upstream: a warm gentle flow, somewhere close to body temperature, smoothing the boundaries of Self, Riverbed, Landscape, Universe. Instead of crosscurrents, it was mirages which prowled the dry bed, spilling up and over, breaking the banks, renting far off treelines like daisycutters, resurrecting them within seconds, endlessly repeating the cycle. Only the

Poole's Grave

coolabah trees arching overhead seemed tethered and permanent.

This riverbed was a stones throw from the tree marked in the mid 1800's as a headstone for James Poole, the only member of explorer Charles Sturt's inland 1844-46 expedition not to make it back. The tree still contains legible initials and a date, carved into the tree by Sturt himself. We stood there by the tree studying the inscription, holding a copy of Sturt's written account of the expedition: the book had travelled nearly a thousand miles with us to be at this location. Here, Sturt's words acquired a new dimension, resonating with the same landscape in which they were written, vibrating on the page as they once again found themselves exposed to the relentless light of the arid interior.

The air here sparked, grounding between present day and a time so recent we could almost touch it.

The landscape here was charged.

No imagination was required to figure why that particular tree was used as a grave marker: (a) it was there, (b) it seemed the kind of place *I* would sure bury a fallen explorer (not far from camp, near a river, a good view of the stars), and (c) it is in full view of Sturt's Cairn, atop Mount Poole: a hand-carted, hand-assembled pile of heavy rock that was built to keep the men occupied whilst bogged down and otherwise unable to proceed in any way other than up. This cairn ended up being a monument to the man who oversaw its construction: Poole.

Coolabahs. I could look at these trees for hours- just sit watching them- and this creek was lined with them, along with other trees and grasses and shrubs I wasn't able to identify. But it didn't matter. I could walk right next to huge, living coolabahs, branches a half metre in diameter lazing down into the non-existent water. I could jump upon them, brush them with my palm, smell them, watch the ants, feel the bark, note the colours, look up three times my height to flood debris snagged way above my head, observe how the clouds appeared above the trees, imagine Sturt viewing them as saplings. I could gather what meaning I could from the stones in the light, and try to feel down deep for the roots which- judging by the sur-rounding land- must have gone down quite a ways.

These trees acted as correcting lenses for the raw desert light: rather than redistributing it via surface reflection, the coolabahs seemed to absorb the light, impart some portion of themselves into it, and throw it all back out into the world as an act of rarified honesty.

.

A dry riverbed, to me, seems always aware of your presence. They never for a second allow you to feel at ease. They seem always to hold their breath. Something, somewhere, is always drawing near.

A dry riverbed is always- *always*- expecting you.

JIMS RIVER

Local River

I saw no unusual thing that day. No bird flew over. I heard no movement close or far in the brush nor any animal call or cry. The landscape seemed as primed as I was for something to happen, though, its edges almost glittering they were so sharp.

Barry Lopez, *Resistance*

Twenty-three years ago this month, a sniper bullet punched straight through Jim Maybetts' chest and out his spine, knocking me off balance as it caught my body armour. It was meant to be a two-fer: bastard had the choke point ranged from a treeline six hundred yards away, had sat there for hours in the hope two idiots like us would line up for him, all nice and single file-like. Jim hadn't died right away, which had made it worse: I had time to crawl over to him and make promises I knew I'd never be able to keep. *I'll take care of your wife. I'll make sure your kids grow up safe. I'll tell your parents you didn't die in agony. I'll tell them you were brave at the end, not terrified.* Sandy the medic hadn't even bothered with morphine: just held Jim's hand, looking him in the eye as he bled out into the rocks and dust. When he was gone, we radioed in the treeline and had a Warthog tear it all to shit. I can still hear the trunks splintering like firecrackers, even from that far away: still see the shrapnel pulverising leaves, branches, human limbs. We'd approached the treeline, hoping for survivors to kill, but the largest part of a human we found were a pair of burning legs, and part of an upper torso suspended from a shattered tree. Later that deployment Sandy was killed by a roadside bomb. The blast that killed him also took my left arm off at the elbow, and deflated a lung. The lung is better now. The arm still hasn't quite grown back.

People look at my missing arm and pretend not to notice it: some even give me a wide berth, like they might catch something. It used to bother me, but I'm ok with it now. I never wanted a prosthetic: I want people to be able to see what happened. The thing is this: the rare occasions that someone asks about my arm are the only opportunities I have to talk about my dead friends.

When I got back from overseas, I lived in the hospital until all my ops were done. My wife- she was my girlfriend back then- stayed with me every step. There was so much misery in that place. It used to piss me off. Other guys, the far worse ones, some of them had almost no visitors, or just sporadic. I felt pretty lucky with my injuries: I can still walk, see, taste, smell, eat, shit, and piss like I used to. Some bastards lost two limbs, or more. I heard of one guy who lost them all. All four of them. So my wife, there by my side all the time- it meant so much to me that I got angry whenever another soldier was unattended, even for an hour.

When I got out, I went to see Jim's wife. She was a wreck. I told her what I'd promised Jim. She didn't want to hear it. She just wanted to be left alone. She died not long ago. Too young. Her kids are all grown up now. One's in the Army, April's her name. The boy, Jim Jr, he's a mechanic today. Was a baker yesterday. Probably be a lumber yard assistant tomorrow.

Anyway I guess the thing I want to say, want to tell you, is what happened the day before Jim was killed. What he showed me.

We were laying around one afternoon and he pulls this photo out of his vest. He'd kept it on him the whole deployment. He had other pictures- shots of his wife and kids- he took these out more or less every day. But this was different: something he'd kept hidden, just for himself. He'd said my name, then handed it to me. *Mitch*, he'd said, *That's me. Twelve years old. And that's the Pinnacle River. That river was my favourite place as a kid: then we moved. That fishing rod, I've still got it at home. I can smell the river on it. I can smell it. I hold that rod, close my eyes, and I can hear the water, feel the shape of the rocks, surround myself with hatching clouds of mayflies and caddisflies and stoneflies. Swarms of 'em. I haven't been there for years, but I can still remember it. When I hold that photo I'm back there, standing in that water. It's all I want to do when I get out of this shithole: go camp on the bank, right there where that photo was taken, and just stand in that water. I want to feel centred in it. I want to feel at home in it. I want to feel it push against me.*

I miss it so much.

.

I hadn't known what to say to him. I've never known a place like that, one that really meant a great deal to me. But that river was like an animal to him. He seemed to know its *personality*. I didn't know how to respond to an idea like that. I did the best I could: I told him it looked like a nice place, a fine spot to camp, and we spoke about fishing for a bit. But I know I'd disappointed him. He'd put some faith in extending this sacred thing to me, and it was clear to us both I couldn't comprehend it.

Still, he was kind enough to not outwardly show it.

I wish I'd known how to talk about that place with him. He did smile after a little while, though, and put the photo back in his vest pocket. And for a minute he was calm, centred: I could see he was back at home, standing in that water, hearing whatever sounds you hear on a river, immersed in the memory of it, experiencing it like he was physically there.

Like I said, that was the day before. We'd sat there all afternoon, propped against a stone wall drinking coffee and Pepsi, watching southbound clouds scudding high over the perimeter fence: reinforcements heading toward battle.

Vignette: 3x One River

1986. Camped by a river in a large canvas tent. I'm five years old.

I'm woken, wrapped in an ex-army greatcoat- swiftly, as if the compression of the night may well crush me otherwise- and whisked outside.

A telescope waits upon a silver tripod. As I wait, its legs are adjusted for height. As I continue to wait, *my* legs are adjusted for posture. Then: right eye pressed to the eyepiece.

I focus: Halley's Comet.

Not thirty yards away, the cobbled stream bubbles up the water, a permanent deep sloughing emanates from a drooping blackwood branch, inexplicable plops and dashes punctuate the starlight.

The last time the comet was here, these trees did not exist.

A river at night is a different beast.

.

The stars are steady.

Darling River

The comet is crystal clear.

Some days later, I view it again, for one last time during its '86 visit.

Some years later, I calculate the age I'll be when I see it again.

I'm half way there now. The gravity of that moment, and those moments, haunt me still.

...

Maybe a decade later.

Camping in an old shearing shed by the same river.

Some other people pull up, another family also camping with us. Have we heard any news? Have the police visited us yet?

These arrivals tell us how they'd been pulled over by a patrol car, just down the road. At first, they couldn't figure out why.

The police had been friendly, but businesslike. There'd been a shooting apparently, a ways off down the road. Had anyone noticed any suspicious activity or anything to be concerned about? Any strange people? Would there be any issue with them having a quick look through all the camping gear? The cops checked the car, found nothing that could contribute to the senselessness of what happened. Thanked them for their time. Moved off downstream: following gravity, and protocol, to the next set of campers.

Some while later, in the paper, we read about the two teens: shot themselves, a response to Cobain doing the same damned thing.

...

The when of it is not important.

Camping in the same old shed by the same river.

Someone brought a new man along, as 'camping would do him good'. The man- detached, unable to focus, broken- was a mystery the whole trip.

We found out later what had happened the year before: four people had wanted to go flying, but there were only three available seats. So- thoughtfully, generously- he urged his wife and two young kids to take the first flight.

Had the aircraft run into trouble on the tarmac, or stalled on final approach, things would have been different. But the damned thing chose to become unresponsive thousands of feet into the air. He knows, because he witnessed it: he suffered the impossibly long, and painfully short, duration between engine failure, loss of control, and ground impact. Watched his family spiral through the air like sycamore seeds, all the way down, watched his wife and kids killed the instant the Cessna corkscrewed into the Earth as if smashed down by a giant hand.

The man- I forget his name- was more shell than human. But there was a being deep inside there somewhere, there was no question of that, for at times there were small outwards signs of life: the roiling convection currents within him bubbling over, threatening imminent rupture.

I doubt the camping did him much good at all.

THE WHITE TROUT

No-one else seems to have seen the sparkle on the brook, or heard the music at the hatch, or to have felt back through the centuries; and when I try to describe these things to them they look at me with stolid incredulity. No-one seems to understand how I got food from the clouds, nor what there was in the night...They turn their faces away from me, so perhaps after all I was mistaken, and there never was any such place or any such meadows, and I was never there.

Richard Jefferies, *My Old Village*

One dark evening, many years ago now, I overheard a conversation between three older men in a rivertown pub.

The day had been tiring for me: up several hours before daylight, a hike into a new stretch of river, a full day of fishing, and a hike out again- by torch- long after last light. I was sitting at a table in the pub alone, exhausted, slowly being digested by a tattered couch whilst ruminating on the number of flies I'd lost to backcasts, when the first scraps of this particular conversation intruded upon my consciousness. I recall leaning forward slightly, casually, in the way people do when they are straining to hear something that is none of their business, and- I'm ashamed to say it- pretended to be oblivious whilst focussing hard on separating the patter of rain and the din of the bistro from the lowly-spoken syllables which fell, like precious sparks of fire, into my life.

One of the older men was relating an encounter he'd had that day with a trout. The way he described it, the fish was elevated above the surface of the river, four feet or so, swimming through the air as if it were water. Apparently, the fish was luminous white, and moved as a trout in water would move: lithe, purposeful, confident.

I was young, and listened arrogantly, condescendingly, my initial aim being to remember as much as I could so I could re-tell it to my mates for a laugh, already tasting the social credit. But, as I continued to listen, something changed. I learned, as the other two men each slowly responded, that all three of them had seen the White Trout at some time or another in recent years. It was always moving, always on a different river, and each time it was headed upstream, suspended above the water. At a very deep and human level, they all seemed terrified of what it might represent: not only the fish itself, but the fact each of them had seen it. I continued listening as the rain and the night bore on, then retired to my room.

I left town the next day as planned, but I never ended up telling my friends about what I'd heard: I couldn't have done so without feeling I was betraying the men. It seemed they grasped some small thread connected to a decisive truth: and, even back then, I knew not to mess with things like that. So I buried the whole experience instead, writing it off as quaint folklore, an artefact of excessive isolation. I left this memory and this idea alone in the mountains, to wither and die alone. If I'm honest, maybe I was a little embarrassed I'd been attracted to the story in the first place.

.

Some years later, I found myself in the area once again. I decided to spend some time asking around about the White Trout, wanting to hear for myself, I guess, that it had been long confirmed a hoax, that those men performed that little pub act as a regular routine to scare away out-of-towners or something. What I heard, though, was more opaque. Everyone I spoke to scoffed at my queries, or pretended not to hear. The few locals that did speak to me regarded the three men I'd overheard as unhinged, even insane: according to them, most people held this view, to the point that the men were now outcasts within the entire district. The men were described as 'river rats': they were living out of cars or temporary bush shelters, shunning society, supporting nobody, ruining the reputation of the area. It became clear that nobody wanted to associate with them, let alone openly acknowledge the existence of their story.

Perhaps, they instinctively knew the men really were insane.

If I'd left it there, if I'd stopped asking, I could have walked away right then and never looked back, and lived an unhaunted life.

But I saw something deeper in the evasive responses of the people I spoke to, their unwillingness to even begin discussing the topic with me. It was as if the townsfolk sensed the core of something too incandescent to observe directly: it seemed they could foretell the consequences of being drawn into an association with the men, reeled in by the story to a point beyond the event horizon. So I left the area feeling confused, foolish and imprudent: but this time, I never let the story go. I couldn't. I simmered on this fish for months at a time, rising to a rolling boil every now and then: the upwelling fragments- the details I had dissected, analysed, and dismissed- consuming me. Eventually though, I could perceive the outline of what I had to do. I cannot take any credit for my actions: there was simply no question of what needed to be done. Determined now, I returned.

.

I allowed myself a week on the water. After careful consideration I'd chosen a river called the Pinnacle: I'd found a bunch of old contour maps, and this stream stood out to me. The first day was a washout: I spent all day whittling driftwood under my tarp shelter by a fire. Day two, a perfect day, clear, constant insect hatches. Seven released fish- good for me, but I'm not a numbers guy. For me, it was about being on the river, becoming something riparian.

And waiting.

The third day, about 2:00 in the afternoon. I was on a wide, sweeping bend, slowly blind casting into bubble lines, down gutters, and around boulders. The thin water around the bend sparkled pristinely in the Sunlight: a glimpse into the furnace of an Origin, as if light was forged right there at the interface between water and hundreds of vertical miles of atmospheric pressure.

There was no wind.

It was while repairing a leader knot that I first noticed the movement. I ignored it initially, thinking it a large bird. When I looked up I saw, not two rod lengths away, a trout of 4lb proportions, phosphorescing pure white, moving upstream just above the surface of the water. The caudal fin worked slowly against the air, the fish moving unhurriedly, methodically, deliberately. I stood petrified, terrified, awed by this creature. It advanced with the manner of a being totally immune and impervious to everything, yet at the same time exuded fragility and susceptibility. Never before had I witnessed such presence, such grace.

The fish continued on, disappearing around the next bend. Shaking, I sat and buried my face in my hands, the implications of what I'd witnessed slowly dawning on me. I remained sitting like that for a long time. Eventually, when I stood up again, it was dusk.

.

I didn't know it then, but I would spend a significant portion of my life trying to get a second look at that fish. It became my singular purpose for existing. It impelled me. It consumed me. I had no idea I would spend so much time searching for the White Trout, no idea how much it would affect me- and, back then, I also didn't know that despite all the searching, I'd never once manage to see it again.

It began right away, really, on that lightswept afternoon. Or more accurately, it never stopped. After seeing the fish I didn't sleep for two days, and then, after finally getting rest, I was out in the field again. Day after day, stream after stream: you may recall the fish had never been seen on the same river twice. I could not continue to finance what, to most people, was an act of derangement- of something beyond desperation- so I sold nearly everything I had, quit paying rent, and gave away anything that wouldn't fit into my car. I became, with alarmingly rapidly, a fringe dweller, an outskirter, someone who kept to the shadows of society when, if absolutely necessary, there was any need to interact with people at all. I was not a recluse, though, as people tended to view me: rather, I was interacting with the world far more intently and consciously than I witnessed others doing within human society. This seemed to be the key factor that rendered me intolerable, an undesirable.

Years into it, after observing how dedicated I was, how earnest and persistent I'd become, the three older men I had originally overheard finally made contact, befriended me, and began to trust me and open up. Our experiences sustained us, kept us on course, nourished our conviction. None of us wished for this path: not one among us felt 'chosen' or 'selected', or even particularly well tooled for the task that required, above all else, a suspension of what we each believed to be physically possible.

The combined depth of field of our quartet began and ended with our experiences, our visions, of that fish. Together, we became something purposeful, directional. We were four tributaries that became a coursing river when our waters combined. We spent years together in search of the White Trout, expeditions that often lasted months at a time: we'd reassemble after each search and, straight away, embark again into the wilderness. And eventually I, like them, became hardened and immune to the scorn and ridicule of the small riverside town, and the villages up and down stream, up and down mountain range.

As the three men aged and dwindled to two, then one, the searching became more frantic, more hopeful, and more hopeless. When the last of them died, I spent a solid year camped on the riverbend where I'd seen the Trout, mourning the loss of my friends, the loss of any remaining hope, and the loss of who I used to be. I emerged from this year defeated, dejected, yet pushed on anyway, making day trips, pouring over maps, reading too much into small natural inconsistencies and interpreting them as leads or messages. Eventually, finally, I gave it away. I realised I had allowed the White Trout to define who I was for nearly half of my life.

I had to let it go. I had to extract myself from it.

I lament those lost decades: I grieve the vacuum of those irrecoverable years.

I've not been back to a river since.

.

I hope you see why I had to share my story with you. I owe it to that animal. I have to make you aware of its existence, and I hope you can forgive me for doing so.

What worries me- deeply- is that nobody knows how to comprehend or acknowledge the White Trout should it show itself again. Nothing in our vocabulary or understanding is able to wrap around the features of this fish, gain purchase, and be propelled by it to helpful or thoughtful actions. We can't begin to correctly identify the lines of inquiry upon which to bear, because in itself the fish offers no grounding place, no tangible nucleation site for such thoughts to form.

I realise now that what drove me to search for the White Trout, and what kept fuelling the search for all those years, was an assumption that it needed saving: needed looking after, protecting, shielding. But now I realise just how condescending and misinformed that perception was.

There may only be one of it, but it does not need our help.

We are the ones who are truly alone.

.

Instead of looking for the White Trout, I now look out for it. I do so by asking questions of myself: What can we do for that animal, to recognise its presence in the world, provide a gesture in gratitude for the fish having made itself known? How do we reciprocate its open handed generosity? Is there nothing that can be offered in return?

I have come upon, for me, the most actively pertinent response I can think of: I go out into the wilderness simply to pay attention. To observe without assumption, to pledge myself witness to the coursings of the wild. I want to be able to show people that there still exists interstitial spaces to be inhabited and explored: unoccupied vacuums linking parcelled scraps of understanding and assumption about the natural world, the Universe, and our place in it.

.

I often think back to that distant afternoon on the river when I saw the White Trout. The quality of light on the wavelets: I can remember that light as clearly as if it was yesterday, the memory of it penetrating the decades as effortlessly as a kingfisher piercing the boundary between water and air. The way that light shimmered and glistened on the riverbend, the way it distorted, refracted, reflected, reminded me then, as it does now, of hefting a crystal whiskey tumbler: the way you can turn it in the hand and measure the clarity of the glass against the transparency of the air, and imagine- if you hold it just right- that objects which are physically obscured by the glass, yet still visible, have been gravitationally lensed around it.

For Marie McInroy

Vignette: Bull Rock

Sometimes, when you have not been to a river for a while, your hunger for flowing water becomes an all-consuming need: your every thought, action, conversation, is in itself a headwater, a tributary, of the river you yearn for. This defined the lead-up to our trip to the Goulburn that year: our first post-lockdown trip since Covid to fish in a stream outside of our imaginations and conversations and dreams.

I recall in those days *needing* water in a way I had never before realised: even rain on the car windshield, impacting and forming rivulets, became worlds of cobble and splintered light and vividly hued trout that I inhabited, dangerously, as I drove to work or sat at stop lights. One night in the shower I realised I'd been staring at my arm for far too long, studying the way the trickle of water negotiated a small scab like a mid-stream boulder, and realising that I had been playing out the kinds of

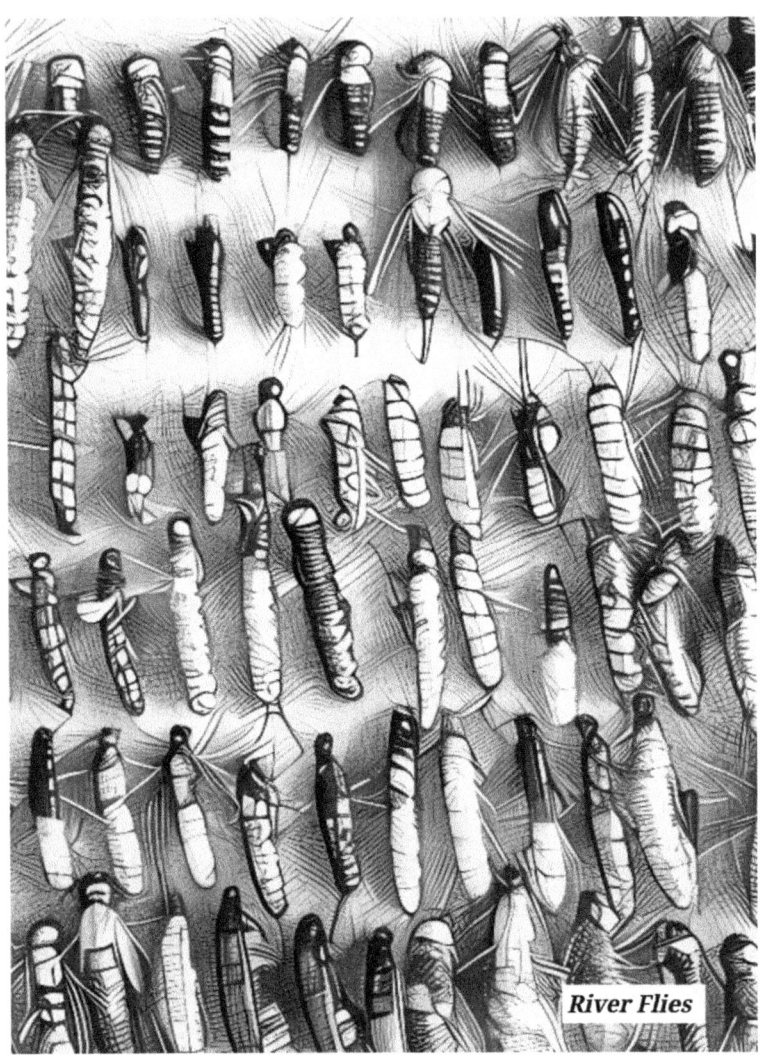

River Flies

casts I'd need to make if I was standing river (shower water) right, targeting a fish in the back eddies of the boulder (scab).

I realised then, standing there, that the situation had gotten a little desperate.

And then things opened up, and trout season was upon us, and we were able to engross ourselves in the planning of a trout fishing trip.

·

Finally on the water, it was a relief to immerse ourselves completely in the riparian world. Our opening day was one of those hot, clear days on the Goulburn where you see a lot of insects, spot some fish, but there seems to be no detectable pattern to anything. Still, we landed a trout around lunchtime. From our old backpack came salt, pepper, paper plates, cutlery, a stainless steel grille. A scaffold of rocks was erected, a fire-lay fashioned and ignited, the grill placed atop, the fish cooked metres from the water, our river-worshipping communion taking place in the shade of a lone tree.

To say we were grateful for everything we had, and that we felt privileged beyond belief to be sitting by that charging water eating our fish, is to not say the half of it.

It was a special day, that day.

·

On the way out, a massive, mentally-deranged Angus bull took to menacing us: the damned thing picked up our trail as we wound our way through chest-high, snake infested weeds. As it got closer, the bull made outward, obvious signs that our journey might be about to get a little confrontational. At that point we were near the river, so I picked up a river-crafted rock to defend ourselves against the foe: something to hurl at the bull in a last ditch effort to knock it out cold, if it ever actually came to the beast charging us. The rock was almost spherical, worn smooth, and heavier than you'd think for its size.

The Bull Rock.

.

Thankfully, there was never any need to employ Bull Rock. That wild Angus must have figured that if two humans believed a palm-sized rock could stop *it*, they must be more deranged than even itself.

It left us alone from that point.

We have the rock to this day. We kept it. Every little while I will walk past it on the shelf, heft it, and think back to that sundrenched day on the water, a day embroidered- like so many riparian days- into my love of wild places and rivers.

THE PINNACLE

Local River

In times like those, the hunter- like the gardener, the fisherman, or the poet- is glowing and burning, and all flaws are burned away, and there is a greater membership in a world that is ancient and miraculous. In times like those, it is possible for the one who burns cleanly to believe that there is a purpose and reason for everything, and that we- improbably- are chosen to be here, and that the greater good within each of us is going to prevail over the lesser parts of ourselves.

Rick Bass, *A Short History of Montana*

If I think back far enough, I can still recall a time when I never dreamt much. Maybe you've known the same: you go weeks, maybe even months, without dreaming. Myself, I usually slept deeply, and after the few rare dreams I'd wake to find the details difficult to recall: sketchy and disarticulated, mostly featuring people I didn't know and wild animals I didn't recognise, doing things I couldn't understand. I'd always awaken with a deep, all-consuming unease.

The night I first dreamt about the river, I knew I'd collided with something important. A river- a small one- picked its way through a bank of fog, the water visible only when, in the shallowest parts, the surface took on the features of the cobbled stream bed. Droplets of condensed fog had fallen from the willows, patting down onto the water, soaking into my woollen hat.

This river dream came back to me every now and then, but because I'd never really been to the forest before, and had no real interest in rivers, I always shook the experience off as an irrelevance, and never paid it the attention it deserved.

That was until the morning I woke up parched, having dreamt that the stream had ceased flowing and run permanently dry. For many days after this dream I could not shake a tangible sense of loss: it shadowed me.

I accepted, finally, what I'd vaguely suspected all along: something significant was at play here, and I needed to stop and pay attention to it.

I needed to locate that river.

.

Not being a real outdoorsy kind of person, I didn't know where to start. First, I bought some hiking shoes. Then I went about making scouting trips into the country and forest, getting a feel for the land. I'd never felt particularly comfortable being out in nature, but still I'd stop and walk around the woods, or wander across a field, or hike five or ten miles through wilderness, rastering the land. I got a sense of the landscape, and found a lot of water: but it was never the *right* water.

Sometimes, in my wanderings, I'd emerge from a gully, or round a bend in a creek, and come up hard against the fence of the mine. I never had paid the mine much thought before: it was simply a place you never went to. But as I kept butting against the boundaries, it became increasingly clear to me that nobody ever went to the mine because nobody was *welcome* there. Even from the outside, this was clear: the fences had been placed thoughtfully, so as to offer absolutely no view of any mining operations, internal roads, or buildings. Instead, all you got to see was the cyclone fence: standard issue 2-inch galvanised diamond holes. Razor wire at the top, both sides. And every few hundred metres, a suite of remotely operated cameras, among them thermal detection systems to spy intruders.

I wondered why anyone would ever be so protective about calcium carbonate.

I'd been searching for the river only a short while- just a few months worth of weekends- when I stopped by the side of the road in the woods one day to rest and stretch my legs. Returning to the car, I happened to notice a section of nearby forest. The arrangement of the eucalypts and dogwood- the sinuous traces of ferns and blackwood, the distribution of colour- it struck me in a very precise way, though I would never quite be able to pin it down. I walked over, paused a second, and slipped into the forest. Within a half hour of picking my way blindly along, I had found my stream.

.

By now, I'd formed real questions about this river. I wanted to know what it *was*. I wanted to see where it went. I walked alongside it, picking my way downstream. At dusk I found myself making a shelter beneath the roots of a fallen birch tree: the second night found me again cradled within the woods by the river, then the third. I had no plan, other than to keep moving. Days accumulated. I continued to accompany the stream as it navigated clay beds, narrow granite ravines, and large dank pools. The river tethered me to the lowest points of the country, so out of irony I named it The Pinnacle River. At night, I would make a fire and lay by the coals watching the stars, imagining each to be a globe of cool flowing water. And, every night I dreamt.

The Pinnacle was there in my dreams from the very first night: I would dream of walking it, picking my way along the cobbles, searching for a path forward. I would often turn and face myself in these dreams, recognising a person accustomed to discontent, hardened to discord. Always, I awoke deeply troubled, in need of rest. Yet the question of turning back never once formed within me.

As the days wore on, I began to notice things, things someone like me had no place perceiving. I observed how the frequency and volume of a beetles droning wingbeats mirrored the size and spacing of leaves along a riparian poplar tree: how when a spiders web flexed in a breeze it took on the billowing dimensions of blackwood firesmoke, how vertical columns of dancing insects at dusk promised fine, stable weather ahead.

My thoughts now ebbed and flowed between the languages of English, bird calls, stream sounds and wind patterns. I recalled how once, long ago, I used to forget my age, and had to figure it out based on what year I was in. It used to half embarrass me. But now, in the forest, I caught myself unsure of my native language. I'd become such a part of the natural world around me that, at times, I wasn't sure what type of being I *was* anymore. I was not bothered by it: in fact, it struck me as archaic that such a distinction could even matter.

.

The real trouble started where everything had begun: in my dreams. At some point of my journey, every dream started with me opening my eyes to a cool pile of ashes, and ended by going to sleep next to a warm fire. You can see my problem: I had no way of knowing if I was asleep or awake, dreaming or actively viewing the world around me. For a while I tried to find out: I marked trees, arranged rocks, cut my finger deeply, shaved my hair, gorged all my food, once dammed the river with cobbles, anything that would allow me to align myself temporally. But my dreams and reality were always mirrored, always indiscernible. I'd wake each day unsure of what was real and what was imagined.

Once I began to accept this confusing state of consciousness, I noticed myself changing in more profound ways. I felt that I was somehow becoming more refined, more honed and attuned, as if I was being crafted into something Neolithic. An unsurpassed clarity defined me. I intuited things I'd never been aware of, never even knew existed. I felt I was starting to achieve the kind of ecological awareness once commonplace for humans long ago. I found I could decipher the passage of birds by studying leaf litter. Food procurement had become as subconscious to me as breathing. Once, I heard music issuing from rocks, and wept.

.

I'm not sure how long I stayed by that stream, and I don't particularly want to calculate it. To this day, however, I rarely know what is real and what is imagined. I have no idea where certainty lies. I have begun to write things down, piece by piece, trying to remember what I have learnt, the things that were shown to me during that period in the forest. Sometimes, every now and then, I can definitely say that I am awake, and those days are the most terrifying of all. I hold off sleep for as long as I can, keep moving, drink coffee, call people, go for a drive, hide notes to myself. But when exhaustion finally takes over, I sleep for two, three days at once. And when I awake, it is just as likely to be within a dream.

I still visit the Pinnacle, but it has long since run dry, both in and out of my dreams. Something about a subterranean collapse of limestone means it now flows underground across a large part of my home region. It re-emerges a postcode or two away, but everything that the river attracted- insects, animals, humans, jobs, the feeding of artistic and intellectual ways of understanding- has gone underground with it.

The mine, for its part, didn't even release a statement, let alone issue an apology.

I often re-trace my original journey along the Pinnacle, walking the dry riverbed as an act of remembrance: of the river itself, not of my own experiences. It's not uncommon to find the aged husk of a mayfly still clinging to a stone, the water marks still visible on the rock, the mayflies long gone.

Sometimes I find a faded yabby claw in the cobbles, or a bird skeleton. I wonder what happened to the water rats, the kingfishers, the galaxiids. When it happened, the underground shift of water was sudden and immediate, overnight. How could the animals have known what to do without any warning? I know that most of them must have perished.

Sometimes, I find the old burrow of a water rat in the dry bank, and I treat it as the location of a great tragedy. I offer a quiet respect, and try to think of a way to tell people about what has been lost.

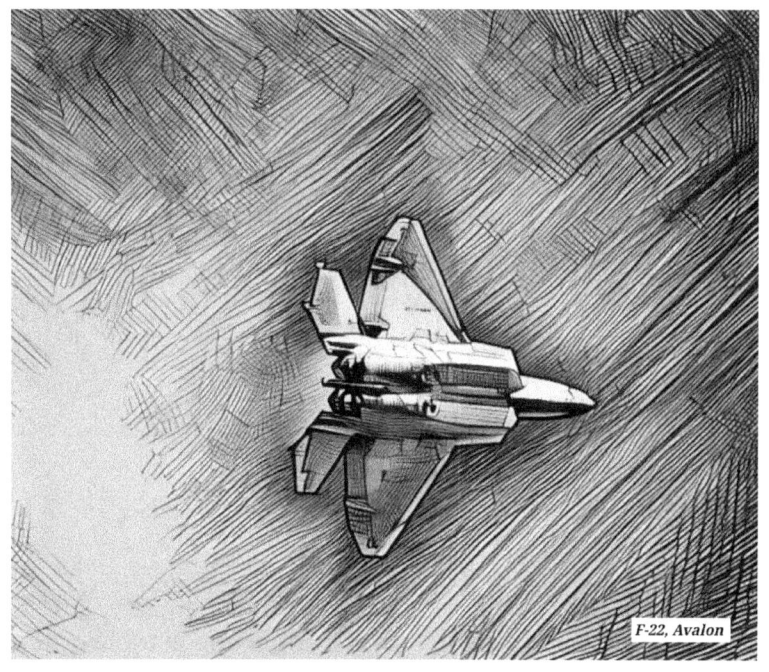

F-22, Avalon

Vignette: Black Sky

B lack flies covered his back: covered them. Homeward bound, still a mile from the farmhouse, way down a quiet pebbled lane, the Summer heat and the flies making the walk home something to endure. We had no idea where the flies had all come from: our best clue was a faint trail of wool far down below in the gully, the wool trail heading towards a thin head-water creek. These gullies were as remote as you could get in this area, and there was always a dead sheep to be found some place or other: and the foxes, without a single exception, always found them first (the flies never far behind them). And often, when the foxes discovered a carcass, they'd move them closer to the creek: maybe the cub dens were there.

I recall wondering, though, why the flies chose *him*.

This was sometime in the late '90's. Later that day, he pro-duced a newspaper clipping. An article about a new plane he'd had a hand in designing, developing computer software for. As an airplane-mad teenager, I read it, re-read it, and asked if he had ever been to Skunkworks. He fired back a raised eye-brow in defence, smiled, and asked "How d'*you* know about that place?"

He would be dead within a decade: pancreatic cancer. An old school and camping and exploring friend of my father.

He was fine then, though, on that walk, on that afternoon, on that steep-sided hill above a gully of half-picked sheepbones.

.

Years later, long after he was gone, we finally got to see his plane. It left the tarmac, flicked to vertical, and punched up, out of sight, lost in the glare of the Sun and a bleached bank of altostratus, the entire crowd awestruck, searching for the invisible source of thunder, somewhere up there in the dazzling light.

It returned, plummeting Earthwards, pulling up into a High Speed Pass, shredding eardrums as the audience gasped, grinned, laughed, cried, tens of thousands of people incredulous and ecstatic. The F-22 performed a Loaded Roll, shot up again, and performed a series of impossible Pedal Turns.

"*That*," I said to my father, my eyes glued to the Raptor, "*is one hell of a goddamn airplane.*"

The heat that day at Avalon reminded me of the shimmering afternoon in the fields on the last day I ever saw him alive, when the flies had flocked by the thousand: with evidence of fox-play written plainly on the hillside, and the creek showing far below as flashes of molten silver.

THE WADER

Space Shuttle Atlantis

O *I see now that life cannot exhibit all to me, as the day cannot,*
I see that I am to wait for what will be exhibited by death.

Walt Whitman, *Night on the Prairies*

Things like this generally reveal themselves gradually, creeping in unnoticed, unacknowledged, like the slow accumulation of mold on a wall: in hindsight, though, her colleagues probably should have recognised the visible accretion of warning signs for what they were. On the day she collapsed, was ambulanced away, and deemed unlikely to survive the night, a collective guilt was voiced: *If only I had possessed the nerve to recommend she go see a doctor. If only I had spoken up. If only I hadn't been satisfied with 'No, I'm feeling fine, just a late night'.* But nobody *had* pressed, and in their own way most people who knew her bore the weight of the occasion personally, painfully, and maybe even justifiably.

Months later, when Petra had returned to work, everyone had understood the unspoken. The aggressive tumour meant two things: her sudden, total loss of vision would be permanent, and her life expectancy drastically curtailed. For most people, it was not hard to see that with her complete loss of vision, returning to the lab was a token gesture at best, and a cruel offering of hope at worst. There was no way that she could continue her work- not without the use of sight to analyse the graphs, formulae, the banks of data, the theoretical models.

And, in any case, she hadn't the sustained energy to keep up with the workload, not like she used to.

Petra understood she had been welcomed back out of pity, and even accepted this truth: but far more difficult to confront was the fact that this field was also her central passion in life. An eminent and respected solar physicist, it was this aspect of the natural world that she was most drawn to. It was not the mountains, animals, rivers, deserts, or birds that resonated with her: rather, it was the measurements, taken by spacecraft and beamed back to Earth, analysed by herself and her team, and then used to make inferences about the composition and behaviour of the solar interior. She'd been an explorer, a pioneer in her field, the fresh scalpel at the cutting edge of natural history and scientific understanding: and now, suddenly rendered unfit for the task, she had been sent back to base camp to wait in the shade while others shot for the summit, did the real work, and made the discoveries. Learning to be content with this- learning through others, not contributing herself- was the hardest of all. She'd never wanted the recognition and awards: she only ever wanted to participate and contribute. To lean her shoulder in and pull her weight. But this past life was, now, far beyond irretrievable for her.

Still, Petra insisted that all recently published papers- from journals like *Solar Physics*, *The Astrophysical Journals*, and *Frontiers in Astronomy*- were read aloud for her: contact binary star systems, globular clusters, solar cycles, stellar magnetism. She insisted on being taken to as many lectures and conferences as possible. She was not, in any way that mattered, about to be robbed totally by this thing.

Mostly, this concept worked. At morning tea her colleagues would read to her, or play videos, or just sit around talking whilst she listened. And so it was that she learned of the discovery of the Higgs Boson, the discovery and disintegration of Comet ISON, and the landing of the Philae spacecraft through interactions with friends and colleagues. The first LIGO detections were explained by two friends swirling their fingers into the skin of her forearm: dancing, inspiralling black holes merging, propagating gravitational waves. Tears formed as this act of generosity had been performed for her.

On days with no cloud, she would use her cane to navigate the corridors, lifts, and stairs leading to the small faculty courtyard. The scraps of en-route conversation pouring out of half-open doors, once seemingly droll to her, were now cradled carefully, nurtured, like injured nestlings. Forming a representation of her world through sound- shaping what she could hear into mental, visual images- took so much concentration and energy that a human voice cutting through all the background clutter (surfaces, machines, air currents, electronic alerts) always made her, in a very real sense, grounded and grateful.

Outside in the courtyard, it was the silence she valued most-nobody ever went there (there was simply never any time for it). Low conversation and scraps of scent carried from the cafeteria- cigarettes, strong coffee, burnt pastries- and she would stand, steadying against a table, and stare right up at the Sun, locating it by the time of day. Petra received no image at all, registered no perceived increase in illumination that would otherwise indicate the presence of the Sun: her world remained blackened. But the reassuring heat of the giant Body she had dedicated her life to: this embraced her in totality, bringing a kind of relief she'd never before imagined possible. Petra envisioned the waves of solar radiation, photons which, having originated in the solar interior and fought for thousands of years to reach the photosphere of the Sun, having traversed the open oceans of space for the 8 minute journey to Earth, were now breaking upon her exposed skin, foaming, the swash and momentum of warm light spilling across the entire shoreline of her face, seeping into every corner of her being, and there, in the vacuum of her unfathomable, bottomless darkness, pooling in rest.

.

Petra could still clearly recall and comprehend all the tools required to explore her corner of Nature- the complex formulae, 3D modelling systems, computer programs, the physical theory. But no longer could she recall the simple fact of what stars actually looked like to the naked eye: no image of a star, not even a generic one, could be conjured. The information was there, but it was simply no longer available to her. The tumour had taken away the one thing she most valued in the world: stargazing, looking up away from the planet into distances too unfathomable, even for her, to comprehend, and marvel at the colossal structures sprinkled everywhere she looked, seemingly unmoving, yet nonetheless engaged in the predictable waltz of stellar dynamics.

The reality of this loss- being unable to form the mental image of a star- hurt her even more than the overarching fact of her blindness, and generated by far the most distress. She knew the vision, the memory, was there with in her somewhere: knew that individual stars had their own appearance to the naked eye: the size, colour and brightness, the way they showed through a cloud veil, or how a bright moon effected them. She knew these things, but could not summon them. She knew that the Milky Way was something extensive and powerful as viewed from Earth, but could not draw any closer to an image than that: no individual stars could be isolated and resolved from her memory of that oceanic inundation of light.

Most conversations with counsellors, psychologists, specialists, and friends centred on these facts. As the source of a great haunting and undermining, it led, like an undercut riverbank, to small collapses: self worth, confidence, feelings of uselessness. And though colleagues were always coming up with new ways of explaining stars to her, the inability to find a place in her imagination to comprehend what they were trying to explain began, after a while, to be a source of unguarded frustration for them. When a co-worker snapped at her, or made an inaudible comment, or sighed, she would excuse herself, seeking out the sanctuary of the courtyard, the embrace of the sunshine. On those days, she would stand there, arms extended outwards, face up towards the Sun, and imagine the inconceivable number of neutrinos passing right through her, continuing on to pass through the entire planet, and continuing on through space, as if the planet was not even there. Sometimes, she took on the perspective of a neutrino: ascending through the solar interior, moving towards Earth just beneath the speed of light, flicking first through her body, then the lithosphere, asthenosphere, the core, and out through the mantle again, exiting the entire planet without interacting with any matter at all. She imagined being that small, that insignificant, that inconsequential: fantasised about being able to pass through the world like a neutrino, invisible, associating with nothing.

Everybody knew her time on Earth was limited. Her motor skills declined- too quickly- but her mind remained edged. When she made it clear she still intended to participate in the annual Conference, the entire structure and theme of the event was quickly altered to be held in honour of her, with a special focus on helioseismology. When she learnt that because of this her colleagues from around the world were scrambling to attend, she did not know how to respond. The generosity shown seemed, to her, undeserved.

She just hoped she'd be there to witness it all.

...

When Petra arrived at the Conference and checked into the hotel for a week, the receptionist- noticing her cane- advised her to keep well away from the river out the back: dangerous path down there for a blind person, she'd offered. The suggestion was coated in something hard to define: condescension or pity, Petra wasn't sure. Still, she had heeded the advice, sticking to the conference hall and dining balcony, never venturing anywhere near the water, needlessly fearful of it. At night, though, she lay awake listening to the nearby Pinnacle, window open, falling asleep to its steady chatter, never silent for even a single second, the river sounds interplaying with random mental snippets from the astrophysical lectures as she drifted off. In this way, a rudimentary image of the Pinnacle formed, revealing itself little by little, illuminated by small scraps of sound:

the patterns, rhythms, notes, and tune of the river revealing the personality and character of the underlying riverbed. Petra began to understand that this river was not dangerous at all: there was an extensively riffled shallow area nearby containing some larger boulders, and a glide a bit further downstream with willows, while off upstream was a plunge pool, a couple-foot jump up to a tailout, then another glide, this one far longer, smooth as a cold windowpane, reaching off to the riffles on the next upstream bend. She imagined floating down the river: could visualise herself emerging from that upstream bend, negotiating the small whitewater leading into the plunge pool, then beaching on the riffled section. Even in her imagination, because of what she had learned by careful parsing of the river sounds, she began to find herself connected to the Pinnacle. She wondered, dryly, if the receptionist had even seen the river for herself.

...

Towards the end of the week, Petra shot bolt upright in the dark one night, heart pounding, fully alert. What was that she had seen? Right there on the edge of sleep: that electrical discharge, that cross-section of a lightning bolt, that image out of frame, just out of frame, yet tangible enough to have woken her? *What had just formed in her head*? She could not retrieve it, and after a half hour of trying, approaching the lost image from every angle she could, Petra collapsed, sobbing openly and uncontrollably. Defeated.

A while later, after a long silence, Petra slipped on her coat, fetched up her cane, and closed the door quietly behind her.

.

Out into the night Petra walked. It was moonlit, she could tell this: there was a crisp feel to the air, there were animals afoot, ducks were shifting about, magpies were warbling, dogs miles apart were calling to each other. She felt ahead with the cane as she headed for the river, identifying where the walking path ended and the trails of animals began. She paused when her cane detected a slight impression in the mud, crouching down to feel the topography of a fresh clean fox print. Closer to the water, Petra heard the tinkle of cobblestones as the fox spied her and shot for cover.

She removed her shoes, her socks. An insect landed on her neck as she searched along next to the stream, a spider web lodging across her face. She didn't flinch: rather, she welcomed the small legs as they moved across her, outlining her form, registering each tarsal claw seeking purchase, surprised at how remote the extremities of her own body seemed to be. The Pinnacle was suddenly loud in her ears, and she sensed that here, in this section, it must be wide and shallow, overlaying what her ears told her with the mental map of the Pinnacle she'd created from the hotel bed. And in her mind, Petra saw not the image she had been seeking these past few months- not the stars- but rather the circumspect path to the image, kind of a mental wormhole that, she somehow knew, would enable the completion of an impossible journey home- should she follow it.

.

The river, here being wide and shallow, had no defined edge: it seeped into the pebbles and cobbles of the bank for metres, the increase in water depth so gradual in these margins that the rocks were only partially submerged. She knew- could hear-that there must be a deeper section somewhere ahead, a hollow of silence out there in the tripping water.

Petra stood on the bank verge, paused a second, inhaled slowly, and threw her cane into the river. She began inching her way forwards over the cobbles, feeling the slow rise of the icy water about her feet. There it was, a silence up ahead: the deeper section. She faced upstream for a moment, as if trying to gather some news from another place, and then turned, walking into the deeper water.

At this time of year, the river was far from warm. In some sections of the streambed the rock was smooth, in other places they were freshly dislodged, collections of jagged edges yet to be worn down. Petra waded in up to her thighs, leaning into the flow, feeling with her feet as she cast about for rocks of different quality, coming upon a raised bed of particularly sharp midstream gravel, submerged under just a few inches of water, rocks so piercing it was not possible to stand in any one place for more than a few seconds. She felt each piece of gravel underfoot as an individual entity: felt the press and painful influence of every single one of them.

Here.

Gently, Petra lay down on the gravel bed, her toes pointing upstream. The water struck her feet and carried around her in a way which, at least at first, isolated her body from the main current flow, the imagined bow seam reminding her of the heliopause. A back eddy formed behind each shoulder, the icy water snatching away bodily warmth, her core temperature dropping, swifted downstream. Rocks shifted beneath her, eroding away, tumbling off into the current, her body settling deeper into the riverbed, the rising water moving past her ears, her cheeks, the cold fire of journeying snowmelt washing around her. It rose into her ears, her mouth.

Where the river had before existed as a series of splashes, plops, plonks, gurgling and sprays, it now revealed itself as a universe of clicking, tapping, sprinkling, knocking, scattering, and knapping: the soundtrack of the submerged world. Petra had never experienced this before: had never put her head in a river. The sound caused her to think again of the constant on-slaught of neutrinos, and how right now, at night, they would be entering the Earth on the other side of the planet, passing completely through it, and exiting her body to continue up into the night sky and beyond. It was a comforting thought she had never realised: that even at night, the Sun still finds you.

Suddenly, Petra felt warm. Comfortably warm. Awareness and consciousness ebbed backwards and forwards, now far away and now within full grasp. In those moments of intense lucidity, her perception of the river seemed superimposed on her thoughts, somehow aligned. Somewhere off in the distance- through a labyrinth of memory, physical sensations, imagery, noises and emotions- she became acutely aware of hundreds of tiny points of sharp gravel prickling her back, the whetted edges patterning constellations of pain and pressure into her skin. Petra tried her best to visualise their positions, to isolate each one, transform the pain from each point into a focussed source, a set of coordinates on a mental map. For a while, her map did not match any star chart she could recall: until one specific arrangement of gravel points unmistakingly resolved themselves into Scorpius. She recalled this constellation, the

THE PINNACLE - 97

arrangement of stars, their names: Shaula, Antares, Lesath. Water continued to climb around her, beyond the reach of her nose, rushing over her forehead, the molecules easily negotiating the human form on their downwards journey to the ocean, further leaching away her temperature, the water washing over her like a mountain wind, the amplified, seething howl of incessant water causing a memory to erupt violently from some subsurface origin, a recollection of a clear mountain evening a decade earlier, further up in the mountains, at one of the headwaters of the Pinnacle.

.

It had been a hiking trip with work colleagues, four days in the wilderness. They had journeyed up the river with no real goal, at one point seizing upon the spontaneous idea of tracing a tributary as it branched up into smaller and smaller rivulets, following the water uphill, to locate the headwater. It was hard work, and pleasurable, and eventually a source was located at the base of a limestone outcrop, the nascent stream seeping from the crushed remnants of long-dead marine life. It seemed so innocuous, that slow, barely discernible trickle: the birth of something tenuous and delicate.

They had filled their canteens from it, sat listening to the glisten of sunlight upon it, watched birds and insects come to take water. They'd camped nearby, not wanting to leave this stumbled-upon place of origin: a place which, for each of them, resonated with something so far beyond articulation that nobody even knew how to begin acknowledging it. For a large portion of that afternoon, hardly anybody had spoken.

They had each of them returned to a place they had never before been to.

That night, Petra had climbed out of her tent to see what was happening in the sky. There had been a strong wind, but the night was clear, full of stars right down to the horizon, even down amongst the treeline. A meteor had appeared, terminating in Scorpius. She'd stood there, transfixed, studying the clarity of the constellation, the way the meteorite trail seemed to linger there before her, not so much an afterimage but an after-event that took quite a while to disappear.

.

The acute pain of the gravel constellation in her back now seemed immediately relevant to that night in the mountains: the sensory information was somehow superimposed upon her memory of the night, the coordinates of the physical Streambed-Gravel-Scorpius embedded within the intense visualisation of the Recalled-Night-Scene-Scorpius, both mental and physical elements forming lenses which aligned and over-lapped, resolving that which had for so long been elusive, inaccessible, dispersed.

For Petra could see the bright red hiking tent pitched on that hiking camp now, herself standing before it looking up at the night sky, could see the exposed pine ridges beyond the other tents, the glowing campfire coals, the dull wash of the Milky Way, the icy mountain wind washing over her face like fresh snowmelt, and right there- suspended beyond the crystalline mountain air- the vivid, striking Scorpius shimmering through the atmosphere, the dull orange fire of Antares, the binary system of Beta Scorpii, the entire vista spread out before her in a resolution beyond imagination, each star in the constellation a point source of colour, luminosity, pain, heat, and texture.

Taken aback by the beauty of this vision, an exhalation of bubbles left Petra's mouth, the current whisking them away, washing them back across her eyelids and forehead, breaching the surface downstream.

As she continued to inhabit the memory of that night scene, she saw the tent begin to dissolve away, breaking up in the freezing mountain wind, the fluorescent red material eroding and receding to blackness, and then transparency, revealing previously obscured star-filled sky. As she watched, the pines too began to decay, the needles and bark and bird nests vanishing in the turbulent atmosphere. Even the limestone cliffs from which the Pinnacle emanated disintegrated, swept up in the watery mountain wind, revealing a final vision, one of such distilled clarity that Petra could plainly see herself turn, pause, and smile beneath the shimmering constellations above, becoming aware that the stars were all there was now: the stars, and the vast chill of space.

Lake Pamamaroo

Vignette: Brookie

The water in the tailout was so unblemished and smooth that it was only possible to tell it was water when taking in the whole picture: the sky, the willows, the riparian bracken, the odd dimple as an insect moved past, the fact that it was more than a struggle to keep from being bowled over by the current. But when all this was removed by cupping your hands to your eyes end on end to fashion a telescope, excluding everything but the water itself, the water surface became the objective lens, and the inverted world existing beyond it- the blue sky, the white clouds, the swallows, the cobbles, the undersides of mayflies and damselflies and dragonflies- became the world upon which you based reality, and within which you injected yourself into. It was a day, and a tailout, just like that: one for the books, one that next season's high water blowout, or cattle-shit algal blooms, or bone-dry, irrigator-bled rotting, non-flowing pools, could never erase.

Days like this are always enough: you don't expect anything of them, you simply inhabit them, losing all track of time, of thought, of place and purpose, allowing yourself to become shaped and morphed by every one of the ten thousand large, small, and invisible things that sculpt the day into being- above all- a perfect day to be on the water.

That's why, when I first saw those dots, I knew this day had achieved next-level status: I'd clocked the system somehow, ran it all the way up, and still, beyond however it is that the quality of days are measured, I'd managed to smash one through the ceiling with what I had on my line.

I was almost convinced, from early on, that it was a Brook Trout. Being an Australian (where there are no Brook Trout in rivers), two things occurred to me: (1) this was not possible, and (2) this was beyond my wildest dreams.

There'd been a bunch of fish rising in a small space within the tailout- say five or six of them- and one of those rises appeared to be different. I don't know how: I can't even begin to explain what was different about it. But it seemed to very obviously have a slightly different quality to it. And so it was to this fish I carefully cast to: promptly landing my rig up a tree. I had to climb the bank right above the rising swarm of fish, and it took a while to disentangle myself from the tree and get a new fly on. But when I did, the slightly-different-rise-making fish was still feeding: and this time, it ate my Klinkhåmer.

It played easily, like a dog on a lead, barrelling in as if I'd offered a treat. But right at the point I saw the spots- I don't know, say 4 yards out- it turned and ran. This changed things somewhat. At that point, I knew it was large- I felt and saw it- but the spots were there too, right on the edge of perception, something I could not be absolutely certain of having actually seen. And, though I had no reason to believe it, Brook Trout was the only explanation for what the snowmelt-filtered light offered me from beneath the surface.

It took a while to bring that fish to the net. Every time it drew near, it spooked and shot out again. I played it very gently, very carefully, the drag set light: I needed to see who this fish was, without getting so excited I ballsed it up and, then, would never know, and forever yearn to *have* known.

When the fish came within reach, I used my net- and missed it- but then the fish was in, and cradled in the water, and- would you believe it!- it *was* a Brook Trout!

Imagine it: an animal you'd read about since you were a kid, a foreign animal, an unexpected animal, right in your own backyard. It was surreal: that's how I'd explain it, surreal. I've read about lions too, and antelope, and condors, and would have had the same reaction had I discovered one of them in the long grass up the back paddock, or in an open field, or in the sky above my house. So it was a gift, that moment: encountering a species I never, for all the right reasons, expected I should ever see in my life.

I'm not a grip-and-grin kind of guy, but I'm not ashamed to say that when a camera was produced, I sure as hell hefted that fish, and grinned like the original Idiot.

In all, from net to release, it can't have been longer than 45 seconds. I slipped it back into the tailout, and it rose to a snowflake caddis two metres later. In small surface windows of just the right angle, I could make out caudal fins, and dorsal and adipose, and the tinge of green and mottled yellow along the body, impossibly perfect in the clear wild river.

I hope, as much as I dare to, that it is there to this day.

I later learnt that Brookies *are* found in Australian waters here and there. A nearby trout farm breeds them, and the fish are sold to private farm dams, and also used to stock various lakes and reservoirs to lure fishermen. It had entered the stream after floodwater provided a link from the fish farm to the river. But a decade on from learning that, I've never once been tempted to try and catch another one. That chance encounter on a Victorian stream, beneath a cobalt sky and above a cobbled bottom of mottled Earthy-browns, was, as far as I'm concerned, my Brookie story.

And I'm satisfied with that.

ORISON/DELTA

Cooper's Creek, near the Dig Tree

For some decades now, it's been a habit of mine to collect a single small stone from every brook, creek, burn, rivulet, river, drain, lake, pond, farm dam, and tarn I have fished in. I have no part in selecting these rocks: that is to say, I never look for them. I merely look *out* for them, and when I meet the right stone (and sometimes I don't), I know I've found it.

Some water I fish is highly esteemed, whilst other places are widely derided and considered downright unworthy, and many streams are unnamed and barely known: but I collect my stones regardless of this, dry the chosen cobble out in the sunshine when I get back home, paint a narrow white-out strip across the back, and record the name of the water on it in black felt-tip. And so I've come to have, upon a shelf in my writing/fly-tying desk, a collection of neatly labelled stones, all around two inches across, from the breadth of my flyfishing world.

I remember how this started. I'd been reading a book about a Native American nation which had a belief that if you were to collect a stone from a place you considered sacred, you would live to one day revisit the site and replace the stone. That struck me as being a particularly appropriate arrangement, and one I could make between myself and the waters I fish: and so, I've been doing this ever since.

As time recedes and accumulates, these stones have become my regular companions. I use the desk daily, and as I craft a Possum Hair Emerger, or Parachute Adams, or a paragraph, the stones (and by extension the rivers they represent) look down upon my work in absolute, almost stone-like silence. And that cobbled silence is the gravitational centre to which I defer when making decisions, the bottom line always being *What is the best I can do for the river? For the fish? For those innately pulled to this place, whether insect, human, or bird?* How will what I am doing- be it crafting Leeson's 'workable deception' destined perhaps to ride in the surface film, or plunge fast into a bank cutting, or survive a thousand Snap C's and Spiral Singles, or be it the obligation to convert these wild places into words, make them known and unknown, such that the place can be acknowledged, defended, recalled and rebuilt mentally perhaps decades, centuries later- how is what I am doing *deserving* of the hundred named and unnamed waters which are all, I firmly believe, sacred places by their very existence? For their part, the stones on my desk and in my hand offer everything by offering nothing at all.

I will often hold one of these stones, measuring its heft, its water-sculpted surface, and try to imagine the history of each accreted mineral and once-free grain of sand and smashed rock and crystal within it- weighing the geological time embedded in this eroded summary of time and place, this product of such immense history and time and pressure that only a *river* really knows what to do with it, wondering if any particles within the stone had once found harbour in other river stones, knowing that four and a half billion years is about as far back as this line of thought can reasonably be enacted: and from there, leap into the immensity of time before these stones even *had* a history, back when the Solar System, the Planets and Sun and Oort Cloud were still unborn components of the Milky Way, back when flowing water on Earth was a dormant idea to be realised somewhere in the vast future of the Universe.

.

Cradling these stones, failing miserably to fathom their deep history, it is impossible not to feel acutely and unconditionally tied and indebted to the riverscape from which the stone was found: to remember the place and hold it close, fight for it, stand ground for it all, for the the river, the stone, and for each tiny piece of conglomerated fawn, viridian, silver, jade, sienna, gold, umber, translucent copper within the stone, every speck of granite, sandstone, basalt, quartz, chert, limestone, each separate grain interacting differently with light, with water, with the forces that created it, slanting human perspective as quickly as the stone is rotated in the hand.

.

Balancing a piece of ablated river on your palm, finding it light as cul-de-canard, heavy as alpenglow, promises are made, pacts are drawn, the agreement lowered gently into flowing water and released to dissolve and diffuse, unseen, to every quarter related even slightly to this river, this creek, this brook, this unceasing flow of *life* and wonder and mystery so profound that we dare not directly probe the subsurface implications of what a surface disturbance might imply.

.

I do wonder how long our journey with rivers will last. It might be that humans will always be around on Earth to witness rivers, recognising and experiencing the deep, umbilical connection between our species and flowing water. Or it might be that rivers will continue to scout and scour downwards, cutting ever inwards, long after the last humans have either ceased to exist, or we as a species have taken leave of this planet: long after the last wars have been fought for potable water, long after most of the fish have disappeared, beyond the time our coral reefs have bleached porcelain, after our ocean food webs collapse, after irreversible disruption to the climate alters water-based systems in ways we cannot even yet comprehend.

···

I have thought much about that evening long ago in the Great Dividing Range- back when I was asked how old a mountain stream was, and if rivers ever die- back when a child made a promise to return to the river one day with a message of love- and about what that all might mean. But even now, I still can't pretend to understand it. I always knew it was insightful- wise even- and certainly heartfelt. But I think now I can at least feel around the edges of why it hit me so hard:

The river was viewed, that Autumn dusk, as sentient: a fragile, living being on a journey to some place mysterious, uncertain, unknowable. Did the five year old want the river to know that it was *ok*, that it was always going to be ok? Was the promise to return a vow to always hold it close in memory? Or a recognition that we, Humans and River, were in it together for the long haul? Was there some comprehension of mortality suspended in there? Was he making a promise that there will always be good people on Earth who care deeply for rivers, simply because in cool, fresh, wild flowing water they recognise an element of nature so essential for human physical and spiritual existence *it needs* protecting? Somewhere there is a boundary where my interpretations of the event blend with my own ideals, and I have to be careful about my line getting too caught up in that particular current seam: but nevertheless, the memory of it has carried through the years intact, unblemished, a small bubble of time I can step into, inhabit and re-live whenever I need to remind myself about why people need to keep fighting to protect the things they love: the people, the animals, and the wild places we visit for the first time and recognise as home.

.

That whispered promise was one of those small moments you sometimes get in nature when the backing curtain is lifted just a little, and through that small crack you get to witness some of the backstage machinery. And what I witnessed was this: as well as flowing ever downhill, rivers also flow into *people*, through people, washing through every artery and vessel and capillary, returning to pour eventually back into the heart, and from there redistributed to the parts of ourselves that need it most.

.

It is my hope- my longing- that in some distant time; in that distant place far beyond the horizon that remains painfully hidden, locked up and unknowable for millenia to come; there may still be found rivers with cobbled bottoms: rivers with water so clear and bright you would swear the streambed was filled with distilled atmosphere. I hope that in this future, among these waters, there would be places that still harbour mayflies, stretches of river where every so often a kingfisher or water rat might make itself seen: a place where, if you were to sit still for long enough, on the right evenings at the right times, you might notice gentle, expanding circles, and caudal and dorsal and adipose fins, and perhaps maybe a mottled body, murkier and more elusive in the water than even the dying light of dusk itself.

And I hope, standing in that distant future, if you could locate a specific glide on a specific stretch on a specific river, and had an understanding of what had transpired there in the distant human past, you could say that

Here,

Many Autumns ago,
Two grown men knelt beside this mountain stream,
Released a stone gently into the water,
And offered,
with open hearts,
an unspoken, river-loving prayer.

Acknowledgements

This book would not have been possible without all kinds of support from a whole bunch of people.

To my fellow authors I have met along the way: your openness and willingness to share skills, knowledge, and expertise with each other is a credit to you all, and makes us all better writers. Thank you especially to Jennifer Comeau, Kate Risse, Stephanie Becker, Moe Claire, Gerald Mercer, Patti Sherlock, Robin Jenkins, Sharon Sheltzer, Evelyn Dean, Albert Connette, Jeffrey Alan Lockwood, and Jerry Kujawa. I appreciate everything I have learnt from each of you.

Charlie Richie Jr at The Backwoodsman Magazine: thank you for your endless support and enthusiasm as a publisher. Your magazine is one of the very best on the planet, a thrill to read, and a privilege to contribute to. Your father and yourself have created a legacy cherished the world over. Thank you for keeping the flame burning.

Thank you to Karen Tropp and colleagues at the Center for Native American and Indigenous Research at the American Philosophical Society for helping me track down cultural information. The time you spent helping me was more than I ever expected.

Finally, to my partner Lucy: thank you for your endless support and encouragement. So many hours of manuscript reading, content revision, cover and illustration design, and talking about the direction and layout of the book have resulted in a work I am extremely proud of. Your countless suggestions helped refine the manuscript and took it to another level. It would not be the book it is without your input.

About the Author

Lindsay Bovill lives in rural Australia, and has been studying natural history all his life. He has formally studied environmental science, natural resource management, palaeontology, and astronomy. His writing has been published in magazines, newspapers and newsletters around the world. When not writing he can be found spending time with his family, exploring Australia, and cooking over campfire flame.

To contact the author, or be placed on a mailing list, please write to lindsaybovill@gmail.com or visit lindsaybovill.com

www.ingramcontent.com/pod-product-compliance
Lightning Source LLC
Chambersburg PA
CBHW070328120726
47909CB00008B/2650